In the Absence of Men

D1190791

VINTAGE EDITIONS

Also by Philippe Besson

His Brother
Lie with Me

In the Absence of Men
Philippe Besson

Translated by Frank Wynne

VINTAGE EDITIONS

2 4 6 8 10 9 7 5 3 1

Vintage
20 Vauxhall Bridge Road,
London SW1V 2SA

Vintage is part of the Penguin Random House group of companies
whose addresses can be found at global.penguinrandomhouse.com.

First published in France with the title
En L'Absence des hommes by Editions Julliard, Paris in 2001
First published in Great Britain by William Heinemann in 2002
This edition published by Vintage in 2020

penguin.co.uk/vintage

A CIP catalogue record for this book is available from the
British Library

ISBN 9781784876364

Typeset in 10.57/15pt Stempel Garamond by Jouve (UK), Milton Keynes
Printed and bound in Great Britain by Clays Ltd, Elcograf S.p.A.

Penguin Random House is committed to a sustainable future
for our business, our readers and our planet. This book is made
from Forest Stewardship Council® certified paper.

Pour Stéphane Cloutour

If you should receive news of my death, this is what you should do. Firstly, you will be and will remain very calm. You will hold your nerve, you will not go about the streets howling your despair; your grief shall be calm and dignified.

RODOLPHE WURTZ
Letter from the front, September 1915

BOOK ONE

OFFERING

1

I am sixteen. I am as old as the century.

I know there is a war, that soldiers are dying on the front lines of this war, that civilians are dying in the towns and the countryside of France and elsewhere, that the war – more than the destruction, more than the mud, more than the whistle of bullets as they tear through a man's chest, more than the shattered faces of the women who wait, hoping sometimes against hope, for a letter which never arrives, for a leave of absence perpetually postponed, more than the game of politics that is played by nations – is the sum of the simple, cruel, sad and anonymous deaths of soldiers, of civilians whose names we will one day read on the pediments of monuments, to the sound of a funeral march.

And yet, I know nothing of war. I live in Paris. I am a pupil at the lycée Louis-le-Grand. I am sixteen.

People say: what a beautiful child! Look at him, he really is magnificent. Black hair. Green, almond-shaped eyes. A girl's complexion. I say: they are mistaken, I am no longer a child.

I am sixteen and I know perfectly well that to be sixteen is a triumph. More so, perhaps, in time of war. Because I have escaped the war, while those just a little older, those who mocked me, have not escaped, and so are absent. And so I am almost alone, wreathed in the palpable triumph of my sixteen years, surrounded by women who take care of me, with their excessive, frightened care.

I love this new century, which carries with it my hopes, this century which will be mine.

Mother said time and again, before the summer of 1914, that to be born with the century was a sign from God, a benediction, a promise of happiness. She was proud of this miraculous coincidence: my birth, and that of the twentieth century.

For his part, father spoke of renewal. I think he used the adjective: modern. I was unaware that he knew the meaning of the word. He is a man of the old century, of the past. He is old. My parents are old. My conception was not planned. My coming was an accident. They transformed this curse – for curse it must have seemed at first glance – into an important, long-awaited event.

I am thankful for that accident, that curse.

2

It is in summer that I meet you. My first impression of you: he is old, he is thirty years older than I. I have nothing to say to you. What could a sixteen-year-old boy have to say to a man of forty-five? And the contrary is no less true. In fact, we do not speak. I know that you are watching me. I do not know what passions I stir in you: envy, desire, disgust, or more probably indifference? I believe you are watching me as you might watch a small animal. I attract your gaze, I cannot hold it. And of course you are a person of some standing while I am no one. People of standing do not waste much time contemplating young men who are no one.

We do not speak. I have no conversation. I would not know what to say to you. I do not even try. Not for the sake of courtesy. Not even to show off my admirable upbringing. Yet I know that a few words would suffice. Good day, Sir. It is an honour. Some such. But I have no interest in playing this game, nor in the rules of propriety. Doubtless, it is indolence on my part. You should not read more into it. There is no stratagem. I do not know how to strategise.

And yet you continue to observe me. Occasionally. From the corner of your eye. All the while giving the impression that you are not observing me. Your eyes sweeping the room and coming to rest for a moment on me. I know what you are up to. I do not give it much thought. I am sixteen. I do not think about a man thirty years my senior.

And then, a voice murmurs: see how the great man watches you. You should be flattered, think of something to say to him, not just stand there like a young man observed. I do not reply. I think: it is the dark hair, the almond green eyes, this skin, so like a girl's. I have nothing else to offer. Nothing to hold your attention. I can think of nothing else.

I make my way to a group of women of uncertain age. They welcome me with exaggerated warmth. I can still feel your eyes upon me. It is decided: I shall not speak to you. I am beginning to resent your gaze. My sixteen years are my own. I am not of a mind to allow a stranger to take them from me. Not, at least, without my consent.

It is summer beyond the French windows. It is sunny and calm. I go out on to the balcony. Almost immediately, you join me in a movement which I sense rather than perceive. Distractedly, or rather feigning distraction, you say: I don't know your name. Vincent. You say: it is a lovely name. I know that you will say this before you do so: it is a lovely name. I turn, so as to see you completely. I know who you are. Everyone here knows you. So I shall not ask.

You say: ask, please. No one asks my name any longer. I comply. You answer: Marcel. Just Marcel, without the appended surname. And I am charmed that you have introduced yourself by your first name. I think we might become close friends, that proffering only your first name has made us intimates, that the cards are dealt, that you are no longer forty-five. I look at you and I think: it's extraordinary, if he had given his surname everything would have been different. Did he realise that by giving only his first name he has completely transformed the relationship which I would no doubt have had with he who bears his name and surname? Did you do it by design?

Of course you did it by design.

You say: this summer is magnificent. One feels guilty for liking it quite so much.

I say: in sunlight such as this one can forget the war. One forgets what war means.

You say: that is a shocking thing to say, you should not say such things.

You think exactly as I do. You forget the war. And I think perhaps you despise yourself a little that you feel no shame.

You say: your clairvoyance is a little disquieting, Vincent.

7

You pronounce my name for the first time. And hearing you pronounce it makes me happy. I like the tone with which you speak my name. And I know that now that you have spoken my name, you will not be able to prevent yourself from asking how old I am. You say: how old are you, Vincent? Sixteen. I am sixteen. You say nothing. There is nothing to say: you are forty-five. You are silent. I have green, almond-shaped eyes, dark hair, the complexion of a girl.

And then, suddenly, you find something to say: so, you are as old as the century. I look at you with a pang of disappointment, of sadness. Not you. This is not how I had imagined you. It is like some momentary lapse of taste. You realise your clumsiness. You try to compensate for it with another clumsy remark: but I imagine everyone says that. Yes, you are right, everyone does, why then do you? Nonetheless, this second lapse mitigates the first. It is a weakness, and in a great man such as yourself, such a weakness cannot but be touching. Then I remember that you are shrewd, that you were shrewd enough to introduce yourself by your first name. This awkwardness might simply be another skilful ploy. The thought, that even your gaucherie might be practised, is seductive. I decide to consider your fault as an attempt to give a faultless performance.

The sun is stronger now. You say: I think I shall go back inside. This light does nothing for me. The warmth, yes, but not the light. I listen to the cadence of your phrase. The warmth, yes, but not the light. I follow you inside, though you did not invite me. Then, suddenly, I notice that you are smiling; you are smiling to see me follow you, though you did not invite me. I allow you to smile, I say nothing. I know I shall have other victories.

We are hampered by our bodies. Here, in this room, in full view of the servants, conscious of the whisperings which accompany your every gesture, we struggle to find something to do, something to say. You hold your head almost motionless. My eyes brush the floor. Something needs to be said; anything but the conventional, else we should say nothing and part. But to be here, like this, not speaking to each other, is senseless. It must stop.

It is more difficult for you than for me. In the first place, you know that you are being observed, that everyone here is waiting to see you get your just deserts, they are waiting to see how you will extricate yourself, how you will resolve this predicament of standing next to a young man of sixteen, saying nothing. You, who are a brilliant wit, a man whose barbs are feared, whose repartee is hungrily awaited, whose every word is dissected, whose literary talent is beyond question: you must find the right words, extricate yourself from this situation. And still you say nothing, you hold your head at that odd, fixed angle.

My silence, my embarrassment perhaps, is easier for them to understand. In any case, next to you I am no one. They pity me, or wait for me to be dismissed. Still you say nothing. I do not feel it is my place to speak first. I say nothing. How long we remain like this, in courteous silence, I do not know. I do not calculate. It does not seem long to me. I feel the silence between us, and I know that in that interminable silence something is being played out. It is our friendship coming into being, taking form. This silence is a bond between us, and it becomes an intimacy, a vow. It is, clearly, a magnificent silence. You relax your posture somewhat. When I look up, I see the trace of a smile. You are overjoyed to have triumphed over the silence, to have made of it something palpable, something meaningful. Those around us who are watching begin to understand. They are thinking: see what has happened before our eyes. A forty-five-year-old man and a sixteen-year-old boy have come together without so much as a word, a gesture. Almost nothing happened. We might so easily have failed to notice, ignored the signs, and yet look: that special bond has formed, grown from nothing, it's spellbinding.

Outside, beyond the open French windows, it is summer still, the sun shines still, a light breeze barely lifts the curtain, there is a warmth, a softness over everything. There is nothing one can do but give oneself up to this summer, nothing to do but abandon oneself, asking nothing. It is enough to accept this summer as a gift, something which one does not deserve, but possesses nonetheless. The floor creaks a little. Conversations strike up again. Still we say nothing.

In the end, you say: I would like to see you again. And in this request everything about your desire for men is apparent. Everyone knows of this desire, it is common knowledge, even if none dare name it openly. Everyone knows and says nothing. We live in a world in which everyone knows and says nothing. You yourself never speak of this desire for men. It exists without ever being expressed. It is there in your request – I would like to see you again – without being overtly declared. But you and I and every person here, we know what you mean. I say: of course. I do not think. There is nothing to think about, the reply is obvious.

You say: come and see me. You give me your address, though I know it already. I will come. You know that I will come. You affect concern that I might not come, but our story has already begun.

Of course, I am not innocent. I am no longer a child. These green eyes, this skin, soft as a girl's, this fragile appearance, this delicacy, are not to be trusted. You should not assume my downcast eyes are necessarily a sign of shyness. I have no stratagem, I have said as much already, but I know what I am doing, I know precisely what I am doing. At sixteen, all things are possible. I deny myself nothing. Why should I deny myself anything?

This is something which you, perhaps alone among those gathered here, have guessed. You have noticed something in my manner, in my comportment, in the sway of my hips. You have noticed what others did not see because they did not think to look, while you, naturally, looked for nothing else. You know that at sixteen I have already bidden farewell to childhood, while still – and in this I have it both ways – offering an image of childhood. You know that the way in which I do not shrink from conversing with a stranger, the way I can strut and pose without a blush, without the least embarrassment, you know these things have meaning. We are the impudent ones.

What is more, you do not underestimate me. From the first, you realise: it cannot be presumed that this boy will not understand what is left unsaid. He will understand everything. There is no need to be explicit. He is no fool. You do not know what will come of our conversation, but you know what to say and what to leave unsaid so that the die is cast. We were meant to understand one another.

I discover that I was meant to be compatible with you, who are almost three times my age, you whose profession is that of 'great man'. I discover that not only does war not thwart life, but that, quite the contrary, it encourages the most improbable connections. Without the war, without this magnificent summer, this absence of men, would we ever have met?

Was I ever innocent? If I were, it was very brief. Very quickly, I think, I began to understand the games of adults: their murmured conversations, their allusions, their risks, their cowardice, their hopes. All too quickly, I was no longer deceived. Something was lost: my innocence, my freshness, my carelessness. I know it is not so for everyone, but I take no credit for this. It was not something I sought, something I effected. It simply happened. And, when it did, I did not think to profit from this knowledge, to fashion it into a weapon I might use. No. I did not add perversity to my precocity. I am not perverse. Perversity demands an effort of will which I am disinclined to make. There is something calculated in perversity, some drive which is not in my nature. I do not seek to set my stamp on events. I let them happen. I simply weigh up their scope, their possible consequences. I am wise to the world and to men.

I realise that I do not endear myself by making such observations. What can I do? I am sincerely sorry. I hope that in this, you will believe me.

3

Obviously, that first encounter with you took place in a salon. One of those salons which you frequent so assidu-ously, in which you stride up and down so patiently, of which, having graced them so deliciously since your adolescence, you have become a symbol, or a caricature. To your friends, you are a man of the world, to your detractors, a snob. I do not judge. After all, I am just like you. At sixteen, thanks to my birthright, the prefix to my name, I have made my debut in society. I wear a morning coat. I observe this human comedy and play my part in it. I am a product of my class, perhaps its last avatar, but I do not feel indebted to it in any way. I do as we have always done in my family, but I attach no real importance to it. I am both insider and outsider. I am neither proud nor ashamed. I am, perhaps, if I may use such a hackneyed expression, sublimely indifferent.

You, on the other hand, sought out the headiness of these salons. More than anything, you sought the com-pany of the high-born, you have been a devoted student, a charming guest, full of wit and prejudices. You have earned your stripes as a man of the world. Through painstaking, relentless effort you succeeded in avoiding *faux pas* and lapses of taste, identified crucial allies, anticipated the fall of some, the rise of others, ensured always that you were in the right place, hoping for some slight recognition, some admittance into this élite, inward-looking, narcissistic circle, feigned some talent, secret or apparent. You made the right choices, those which made people forget that your birth was one rung too low, just one rung, your name which has no prefix, and something else, excuse this dreadful term, something akin to heresy. I am not judging you. I have no opinion, really. I watch you, in your morning coat, gliding through this unreal world. And it occurs to me – like a revelation – that you are not content with this superficiality, that you have begun to dissect it, that you are performing the autopsy of an era.

I like this idea, that having so desired to be a part of this world, you will be the one to write its death certificate. You will do so with elegance, no doubt. I have come into your life just at the moment when you have become a clinical, lucid and melancholy witness to your own past. I walk beside your funeral cortège.

This too is what attracts you to my sixteen years: I am your last connection with youth just as life seems suddenly, dangerously short. And, no doubt, you see in me something of what you once were.

I want to tell you, Marcel, that I accept the challenge

to be all of these things, that it is an enterprise I find interesting, that I have no fear of being everything that is expected of me; every situation is an opportunity for me. I never hoped, never imagined that this might happen, but I am preparing myself to embrace it. After all, why should this summer of all tragedies not also be a summer of all comedies?

A messenger brings your note. You write: I hope to see you on Monday at 6pm. It is like a *billet-doux* that you might write to a mistress, like a love-letter. And it is as such that I receive this pretty paper darkened by your graceful handwriting. In these few words, in the 'hope' which you express, I perceive your taste for young men and the undeniable delicacy with which you express that taste. Not that I do not suspect you of certain turpitudes, a penchant for more intense sensations, less respectable feelings, but I know too that you consider it necessary to appear sophisticated to those in your milieu, or – but of this I cannot as yet be certain – to those with whom you would like to form an attachment. And, naturally, I am happy to give rise to such a hope. Then again, you know only too well how little you risk. You know already that I am neither shy nor naïve, that I will be there at the appointed hour. Since our magnificent silence in the midst of the salon before the watchful crowd, I have a passionate desire to know what twists and turns this story will take.

Father declares himself proud: he reads your articles

in *Le Figaro*, he is a fervent reader of *Le Figaro*. He thinks: my son has succeeded in attracting the attention of such an eminent man. He cannot imagine what it is in me that might have attracted your attention. He sees nothing. He has never seen anything. He is foolish enough to go as far as to crow to his relations about our next meeting at your apartment. His ignorant enthusiasm is met with an embarrassed silence.

For her part, Mother is more reserved. She knows what there is to fear. She has heard the gossip and heeded it. But she is silent. She has spent her whole life in silence. Why should she speak now?

I hear them without really paying any heed. I regret the impulse which brought me to mention our meeting to them. I regret this gesture, which was sheer vanity. And then, the regrets pass. Their opinions matter so little to me. Their wishes are of so little importance. Their reproaches and their encouragement of such little consequence. None of this is very serious. In fact, nothing is serious.

You receive me in your bedroom. At first, I think: really, how shameless, you could be a little more subtle, a little less indelicate. You notice my surprise, my disappointment, my disapproval. You think: he does not know me as well as he might think. In truth, he does not know me at all. You explain: I have spent my whole life in bedrooms. Bedrooms in general, and in this bedroom in particular. It is here that I receive my guests, here that I dine and here that I write my books and my pieces for the press, here that I read and, incidentally, sleep. I say incidentally because, as it happens, I sleep very little and always at such times as others are awake. Do you believe me? Yes, I believe you. I believe this improbable tale. You say: in fact I write books about bedrooms. My novels are filled with bedrooms. They are my memory. It is in bedrooms that everything begins. I listen. I say nothing. You have decided to speak. I follow you through your bedrooms. I learn that it is here that one talks, here one rests, here one sleeps, here one dies, here that one finds oneself alone, or with another, here one dreams. And suddenly I am thrilled that you have received me here and not elsewhere. I realise that to be received elsewhere is a mark of your indifference to your guest, or a sign of his imminent fall from grace. I am almost angry with myself that at first I was suspicious, reproachful, disbelieving. You say: that is what it means to be sixteen. One does not yet recognise the codes and conventions, one is quick to misconstrue, quick to judge. But you will learn. I look at you and I say: yes, I learn quickly.

You say: how I would like to have met you in Cabourg, at the Grand Hotel. What a glorious place for a meeting. There, too, I would eventually have led you to my bedroom. Oh, you must visit the Grand Hotel, the grandeur of the foyer tending towards the opulent, the women hiding their faces behind their parasols, the exquisitely behaved children, the tortured adolescents, the whispered conversations, the subtle glances, the view of the sea, the blue of the sky, a whole world slipping past. You continue, speaking for yourself rather than for me: it is extraordinary, Calvados, Normandy. It is my childhood, of course, but it is habit, too, a luxury which I permit myself, a fixed point, a comfort. Do you know that, before the war, for eight years I spent every summer in Cabourg? It is summer now. I should be there. I should have met you there. Finally, you ask me: do you know Cabourg? No. And then you are off again to the enchanted world of Cabourg, to the magic of this little seaside resort, transformed by the construction of the imposing and opulent Grand Hotel. You talk about the promenade, the fine sand – for it is well known that the sand at Cabourg is finer than any other – of the bathing huts, the casino, of the dandies who make up the strange society of seaside towns. And then you talk about the sea. You are tireless. You say: one should write only about the sea. Nothing matters but to write of the sea. It is difficult, you cannot imagine how difficult it is to write about the sea. I listen to you in silence. I remember your silence at our first meeting. Your loquacity is a surprise to which I will have to accustom myself. I can understand that you are sorry not to be in this place for which you have such a special affection. I realise too, that this tendency to monopolise the conversation is a sign of your timidity, a fear of engaging me in real dialogue. In a way you are prolonging by various means this silence between us, this moment in which we do not exchange thoughts, in which we do not come face to face. You are afraid of our intimacy. You prefer rather to fill the space. I say nothing. I look at you. I do nothing else: I say nothing and look at you. Neither of us is taken in. Perhaps we are not yet ready to find ourselves face to face.

And just as certainly, you are trying to impress me, to remind me of your status as a great man, of the privileged nature of your existence. You set out markers. You set the scene. You are right to do so. It is best to know with whom one is dealing. And I should concede that this is a clear, considered, inventive attempt at seduction.

After barely an hour you dismiss me. You are awaited elsewhere. It would be utterly inappropriate to let them down. The guests would be terribly upset. Your voice rises so much that, as you utter the words 'terribly upset', you sound for a moment like some society harridan. And why do you need to revel in it so? I dislike this affectation. I say: I could be your friend if you will consent simply to be Marcel and not his caricature. You look at me, taken aback, as though winded, as if to say: no one has ever spoken to me as you have, no one has the right to speak to me as you have. But you have the intelligence not to say this. You know that if you do, I will walk through the door and we will not see one another again. You hold back: there – my first victory.

Weakly, you declare: I should like to be your friend. Suddenly, you are like a small boy. You are incredibly endearing. And the hurt I see in your eyes is like a confession. I do not resist my urge to kiss you. I do this, this astonishing, unseemly thing: I kiss you. I had planned nothing. I simply give in to this unthinking desire. I kiss you, and I say: so then I think we shall probably be friends, Marcel. I say your name for the first time, and the sound of my voice sounding your name is as strange and pleasant to you as it is to me. Now, you are completely taken aback. In a few short seconds, a few words, I threatened you with a permanent separation, I kissed you and I called you by your first name. It is too much to take in all at once. Clearly you are not used to this sort of situation. You are distraught that it is beyond your control, you who endeavour to control every situation. You do not know how to respond, what attitude you should assume. I retain the initiative, saying: I shall leave you, I would not wish you to be late, Céleste will take me home, we shall see one another soon. Outside in the street, the light is beautiful. It is the light of late summer afternoons. I think of you, standing there in your bedroom, with the mark of my kisses on your cheeks. I smile.

4

The war is here. It has your face, Arthur.

In fact that is what you are, Arthur, a war erupting into the indolent life of a young man of good family.

This eruption is like a violation, a surprise. I am unprepared for this, ill-equipped to deal with the horror of war, the suffering of a soldier, a world drifting away.

The war was something unreal, something which we kept at a remove from our lives. The war was something far off – a hundred kilometres or more – something immense, remote, which raged in the countryside, in lands that are no longer ours. War was something illusory which did not in the least prevent us from frequenting theatres and restaurants, from living our everyday lives. War was a whisper, an ugly rumour, a passing irritation, a regret swiftly quashed, a pang of conscience with which we could quickly come to terms.

I am not responsible for this war, I want nothing to do with it, I want it to respect my childhood, safeguard the affection of those who are here still, I do not want it to hinder my relationship with Marcel.

And then you turn up in my life, Arthur, unannounced, without so much as a word of warning, dragging with you this terrible procession of bodies, of bombs, of mud, the horrors you have experienced, the mute pain of things which beggar belief, beggar description. Here you are, suddenly, standing before me, wearing the uniform of your twenty-one years, looking at me with your sad, tired eyes, so tentative in their reproach that I would rather they were straightfor-wardly reproachful. Here you are, and you say: take me in your arms so that life can be more than the terror of death which drives us mad, the endless, excruciating wait for death to come. Take me in your arms so that I can be something more than a muddy soldier, an anonymous refugee from the trenches in northern France, a dirty grey shadow. Take me in your arms so that I can feel light, warmth, softness, everything we have forgotten, everything we have lost. Take me in your arms – without thinking, your body against mine, your mouth on mine, give me your milk-white skin to kiss and to caress.

And, of course, I take you in my arms.

You are Blanche's son. I have known you for ever. I do not know you at all. You are the governess's boy. I know your name, your face. I have watched you grow up before me. I don't know who you are. I don't think I have ever said a word to you. You are twenty-one. It has been two years now since you went away to war. Two years since your existence was reduced to a mother's tears, your mother, a mother who wakes every morning to the fear of a telegram and a murky formal photograph which says nothing about you.

Our lives have nothing whatever in common, they never could have. Why then should they suddenly collide today, in the madness of these years of fire and steel? This is something else for which I am unprepared. Something else which I did not anticipate: your imperious demand that I take you in my arms.

You say: I have known for a long time. I knew before you knew yourself. I watched you, secretly, silently, as the pieces fell into place even before you were aware of them. My need for you came with the war, the day I went away to war. I needed an image to cling to. And the image I found was you. For two years that image has been with me. It never leaves me. It helps me through the unthinkable horror. It is there with me, always, wonderful.

To me, above all else – and you can't begin to imagine how much else there is – this war is my love for you. My solitary, solar love which has been growing for two years, for a thousand years.

I don't know if I can explain why I have decided to tell you this today. Maybe I'm more afraid to die now, maybe the danger feels more immediate, and so I need to talk, I need to say everything before I die, I cannot die carrying this secret, this amazing secret. In any case, it is more than I can bear, more than any man could bear, I can't stand it any more. Maybe I need to talk so that I don't go mad.

You say: it is a desperate act, but also an attempt at escape.

I say nothing. What could I say?

You surge into the space between my arms, and the first thing that I embrace is your pain. I hug the war to me, the smell of war, its rigidity like a block of cold granite, like a corpse. At first, the feeling frightens me. I have to stop myself from pushing you away, from giving in to my fear. I am sixteen. I know nothing of bodies, but I know, something learned an eternity ago, that when you embrace a body it does not have this stiffness. I gauge exactly how much this body has been assaulted, cut, bruised, how it has learned to protect itself, to harden, to shut itself off from the world. I gauge the solidity of two years of lead. And you, of course, you understand everything. You know exactly the nature of your offering. You know what it is to be afraid, to be distraught, to be helpless. For two years, your body has known nothing but cold, danger, conflict. But you know, too, that I will not reject this offering, not at all, I will welcome it, you know that I am perhaps the only person who can make it welcome. And yet, it is strange that you should have chosen someone so innocent, someone who does not know the gestures, who has never held another body, a virgin child. Yet you are right to do so. This first embrace must be as it is. It seems suddenly obvious. And so I warm your body, I give it my warmth, I bring it back to life; through me your skin becomes softer, smoother, gentler, flushes pink. Even our tremblings, our quiverings are a warmth. The moment is lingering, slow, tranquil. Almost nothing happens, only this silent embrace. And this almost nothing is everything. It is vast. It is life itself. It is your return to the land of the living. It is my baptism. What has happened feels somehow sacred, somehow miraculous.

We stand there, unmoving, for a long time. We are standing in the middle of my bedroom, at the centre of the world. We are motionless and alive. We are at the essence of life itself.

I feel my heart beat against your chest. I run my hand along the nape of your neck. Your hair is short, blond. This is a gesture I know, one which comes easily, the gesture you are waiting for. I feel my heartbeat quicken just a little. I am not afraid. I am not afraid.

Then, our mouths find each other, our lips touch without impatience. Two years you have waited for this moment, and yet you are not impatient. It is as though you knew that this moment would come, inevitably, that you need only wait. I am sixteen. You are kissing a sixteen-year-old boy, with green eyes and black hair. The kiss tastes of salt. There is a cut on your lip. My lips cling to this cut, falter there, move over it, then seek out the most injured part. It is a gradual progression. I am a path.

Our clothes fall to the floor. Our naked bodies face each other. War has shaped this body, transformed an adolescent into a man. Between my sixteen years and your twenty-one, between my slender torso and your solid chest, is the full compass of the war. You take my hand. I follow where you lead, to somewhere I have never been.

I slide my hand into the hollow of your shoulder, to the centre of your chest, on to your smooth stomach. With the back of my hand, I touch the soft, silky skin of your sex. Instinctively, I understand everything. This entangling is the easiest of journeys. Closing my eyes, I think: truly this is a magnificent summer.

5

In the morning, you are huddled up among the sheets. I imagine soldiers in the trenches sleep and wake in this position, vainly trying to protect their bodies from a bullet, a bomb, from the cold. I realise I have never seen you in your blue uniform, stained with mud and with blood, huddled in your narrow strip of trench, in the terrifying silence of waiting. To me, you are a young man, his skin bare, fresh, tangled in my sheets after my first night of love. I reach out my arm simply to touch you. You shudder but do not wake. I let my palm gently stroke your hip. Day broke some hours ago. I do not dare drag you from your sleep, from your rest.

Later, we talk. You say: we thought we were just heading off for the summer, to fight an enemy we thought was wholly in the wrong; we thought we would return victorious, hailed as heroes by our own. What happened to us? You say: you should have seen it, you should have seen the send-off, the cheering crowds following us to the train, everyone joyful, clapping and shouting, cheering us on, it was like a festival to the triumphant sound of the 'Marseillaise'. And we let ourselves be carried along by this euphoria, by this ceaseless, confident uproar. We were a little afraid, of course, but no more than that. We were arrogant, sure of ourselves. We were fools. We were quickly brought down to earth. We had abandoned everything, right in the middle of the harvest, after the magnificent summer of 1914, but we were in no doubt that we would be home before Christmas. To wage a war and to win a war were one and the same. We couldn't begin to imagine the calamity that was about to rain down on us like a cloudburst. I say: I remember the euphoria, the crowds, the fanfares at the send-off. We were all allowed to go to cheer our future heroes. It is true that for me it all seemed like a joyous celebration. When you did not return as quickly as they had said, everyone fell silent. We did not speak of it, of your prolonged absence. We skirted the subject. And when at last we began to speak again, we spoke of other things. We tried to forget you. You say: I know. We all know. And we haven't forgiven you. You are right. There can be no forgiveness for this collective cowardice, for the individual cowardice of each one of us. I do not ask you to forgive.

You say: I had decided to stop loving men. But you, you are different.

You say: I don't remember what it was like before the war. My memories begin in the summer of 1914. Everything that came before has been lost. Tell me about it.

I say: what good would it do? You say: memories shouldn't only be of suffering. I say: before the war was the *belle époque*, a sort of golden age. In years to come that is what the history books will call it. It was the most glorious decade. Paris glittered. In my memories of childhood, the first thing I see is Paris glittering. But my memories are not those of everyone: I was born to riches, here in the west of the city, here, in the light. Others would doubtless tell a very different story. You say: I would tell a very different story.

When we fall silent, I realise that you have returned to your sadness. Your sadness is a place which you inhabit. Sadness is a geographical reality.

I cannot join you in that sadness, it is impossible. Millions of you know this sadness, but not I. I do not even try to imagine this sadness; to do so would be absurd. I am elsewhere, that is all. I do not resent the fact that I am elsewhere. Nobody could resent me for it. I am in your arms: this is all I know. I have this extraordinary knowledge, this knowledge of the space between your arms. It is my happiness. Happiness, too, is a geographical reality.

When you speak again, it is still of war. You say: how could the assassination of an archduke in Sarajevo, of itself, set off such barbarity? I say: I suppose it was already there, the killing was simply the spark which lit the blaze; the hatred between nations had taken shape over years and years and suddenly exploded in that summer two years ago. You say: this nationalist hysteria is inconceivable. I have become a pacifist. I ask: were you a warmonger before? You reply: anyone who has not been to war is a warmonger; I'm speaking of myself. And you add: I shouldn't be having this conversation with you. I say: because I am sixteen? You say: no, because I am in your bed.

We do not part. We cannot bring ourselves to part. It seems impossible for us to separate. We are new lovers. We are exhausted and happy. How long we stay in my room, while the fierce light of a glorious day filters through the louvred shutters, I cannot begin to reckon. How long we lie together in the sheets as they soak up our smell, our heat, I could not really say. I know that it could last a lifetime, that it could last until the end of this war, that it could last until evening. It is a madness, a fit of passion, something overwhelming. It is a revelation, a predestination, something which demands to be felt. It is a pleasure, a sweetness, something which makes one want to cry. I listen to the rhythm of your speech. I say nothing. My eyes are wide open. Sweat beads on my forehead. My attention is fixed entirely on you. There is no space for anything other. I say nothing. I do not want to say something which will not measure up to this experience. You are the first man.

Later, you ask me: do you know that what we are doing is an outrage? I am a soldier. You are sixteen years old. The outrage is entirely contained in those two sentences.

I have no sense of any outrage. I do not know what that is. It simply does not come within my frame of reference. I am the imperturbable child. I have no moral code. And if I had, I am sure this act would not offend it. I say: what we are doing is not an outrage. You must not think so. That would be a false logic. And it is futile. You say: you cannot convince me that what we have done is not shocking. It will be shocking the moment it is known. We must keep this secret if we are to safeguard what we have. The thought of keeping this secret delights me and I agree at once. You smile at my obvious delight. And in your smile I see a world is born. I stroke your blond hair. I embrace your youth.

You say: I must go. I have to go to my mother. She has waited for me with mounting terror all these weeks. She has shed every tear in her body. She is crushed. She has lived with the knowledge that at any moment she could lose her son. She has lived with this terrible knowledge. For a mother to picture the death of her son is more than anyone should have to bear. It is the most terrible loss. She could not survive it. A mother never survives the death of her children. Though they are alive, they are dead. When she saw me come home, she wavered for a moment and then collapsed. I watched her body slump and fall. A slow fall she could do nothing to prevent. In an instant, all the hours spent waiting, spent in fear, came together and dropped like a weight on her shoulders, crushing her. She did not resist the weight, the compression of all that time. She cried, of course, when I helped her up. She hugged me to her as though for the first time; as though for the last time. She hugged this improbable survivor to her. She covered me with kisses. That is precisely what a mother's love is – that over-powering emotion, spilling as a river overflows its banks. I didn't cry. It was important not to cry, not to add my distress to hers. Already I dread the moment when I have to leave. It will break her heart, it will be painful beyond words. She will imagine that she is let-ting me go to certain death. Instinctively, she will imagine this farewell embrace might be the last. She will won-der if she will ever again be a mother. Such a situation can only be conceived in war. Think it over: there is nothing else. Nothing as grave as this. Nothing whose consequences are as terrible. I have to go back to her. But I want to see you again soon. I want us to spend tonight together. I want us to spend every night together until I leave. The days cannot be ours, I owe them to my mother. So, we must have the nights. I say: I will wait for you. No matter what time you come, I shall be here. When you eventually walk out of my bedroom, I feel an emptiness.

Father says: you were seen with Blanche's son. You know how fond we are of Blanche, how much we appreciate her. In fact, she would hardly still be in ser-vice with us after almost twenty years if we didn't have some small affection for her. Her son seems a fine lad. He is honest, hard-working, he has been educated – I believe he is a schoolmaster – and is doing his duty as a soldier to defend his country. But you must understand that these people are not of our world, and it is important that we keep a certain distance from them. We have always opposed this kind of contact between the classes, this social mixing – no good can come of it, believe me. I feel obliged to discourage you from seeing the lad again, do you understand? This may seem a little harsh now, but later you will thank me for helping to preserve the purity of our class. I do not answer. To my father, this silence amounts to acquiescence. I make no attempt to contradict his repellent convictions.

Mother, for her part, can accept such friendships as these turbulent times create. She is happy that her son is not alone. She says: the solitude of wartime can be very destructive. You shouldn't deprive yourself of the company of people your own age. She could not possibly guess the nature of the company I keep with Arthur. I am grateful for her encouragement, and for her naïvety, which merely typifies her stupidity.

In the late afternoon, I receive a message from Marcel. It is another invitation. And I am pleased that he has asked to see me again. It is a simple, unselfconscious pleasure, completely unrelated to the extraordinary adventure which I have begun to live with Arthur. I am not ashamed of this sincere, spontaneous pleasure. I feel neither guilt nor shame. Nor do I have the impression that I am betraying one or other of my men. They belong to different worlds, to discrete moments. I know that I can love them both. I know that it is not impossible, irreconcilable, that, on the contrary, it is a necessity, a fact. Needless to say, I presume that I should not speak of one to the other, that to do so would doubtless be incomprehensible, unacceptable, at first shocking. I already know that I shall say nothing, I know that I shall not find it difficult to be silent. I will perhaps regret being unable to declare myself, to explain myself. But such regrets are trivial compared to the great happiness I feel in being close to these two men who are completely different, which everything sets apart, whom everything separates. No, I am no traitor. Yes, I am a young man of sixteen, with no inhibitions, who does not divide the world into what is good and what is evil, who believes he has no need to choose between the agreeable conversation of an ageing writer and the delightful body of a melancholy soldier. In my bedroom mirror I face my reflection. I see my black hair, my green eyes, the hint of a smile.

I send a message to Marcel. I write: let us meet tomorrow, at 4pm in the café on the boulevard Saint-Germain I am so fond of. Let us meet, dear friend, for already that is how I should like to think of you. I write to him thus, and I know he will be there.

When I see Arthur again that evening, I can tell that

he has been crying. I see his reddened eyes, his face lined by his tears, by his terrifying sadness. I say nothing. I wait for him to speak. It must come from him, nothing must be said which does not come from him. He remains silent for a long time. It is a still, continuous silence. I take his hand in mine. The palms of our hands touch, a gentle pressure. His eyes stare out at nothing. I do not release his hand. I curl myself about him from behind, my stomach pressed against the small of his back. I lay my cheek against the nape of his neck, the sweet smell of blond hair, on the sweet softness of his pale skin. His heart beats regularly. All is calm, tranquil. Then he turns to me. We face one another. Our faces brush against each other. You must imagine the magnificent madness of two men's faces, so close to one another, that intense sensuality. The kiss is simply a logical extension of this proximity. When our mouths lock together, the suffering seems to dissipate, to disappear. Our minds are fixed on the kiss alone. Nothing exists but this kiss. It fills all space and time. It is the sum of two lives. His lips taste of salt.

6

Naturally, you arrive late. And in the café your very entrance is an event. Everyone knows you here yet no one dares approach you save with a furtive glance, a distant nod, a polite word. The waiters seem to have begun a sophisticated ballet, gliding from table to table in their black and white livery, creating an aura, an invisible circular barrier, around you. Everyone is surprised at my presence within the circle. There are those who have no idea who I am, those who have heard tell of an encounter at the Marquise de V's salon, who intimate that I was the focus of this encounter, there are those who know nothing but speak as though they do and those who were present at that first meeting who alone can reveal my identity: Vincent de L'Étoile. I know precisely the rumours which have begun to circulate across Paris, and I don't think that I care. Worse: I know that this public display will lend this rumour credibility, will make of it a truth, an established fact. And this, indeed, is the substance of your first remark: you cannot be unaware, dear Vincent, that our meeting today in such a public place will be the subject of much speculation in certain circles; that within hours your reputation will be made. Of course not. You are perfectly aware of such things. In fact, I imagine you arranged this assignation expressly, that the situation amuses you, that there is in this no little provocation. I say: it was not at all premeditated. All that matters to me is to see you. You say: the worst thing is that, suddenly, I believe you are sincere. You truly are an angel. I listen to you say this: you are an angel, listen to you speak of my angelic qualities and I realise that it is possible to be someone's angel, that I am your angel and could never be an angel to another.

You say: I find your precocity charming. At sixteen, I was simply a son. The son of a great doctor – did you know that? Matriculation, university, the *Académie*, all of these weigh heavily upon a son. I remember him as a shadow falling across our lives, a man who was greater than any one of us, though none of us would ever know whether his greatness was a blessing or a curse on our future selves. Now, doubtless with the benefit of hindsight, I would say that our indifference was more feigned than real. In truth I learned much from my father. The stories of our apparent loathing of one another are simply nonsense. True, he was a scientist and I am a man of letters. True, he had a fearful temper, while, asthmatic that I am, I am by nature peaceable. True, his love was for the republic, while I delighted in the salons of the aristocracy. True, he was among those who condemned

Captain Dreyfus when I was one of his rare supporters. True, he never truly understood me, and I am not sure that I ever truly loved him. But there was an affection between us nonetheless, something like the memory of a filial devotion. Besides, time heals all things, it leaves at the surface only those images which we wish to preserve. The images I have of my father are not in the least unpleasant. And I am too old to bear grudges. Then, you ask me: tell me about your father. I say: there is nothing to tell, really. We are not of the same world, and I truly believe that this fact causes neither of us any great pain. You say: how marvellously cruel youth is, capable as it is of making the most absolute condemnation seem as if it were the most trivial of things. At this, you smile. You are wrong, Marcel, I did not intend to seem malicious. I wish only to tell you the truth about my relationship with my father and, if truth be told, I have none. You look at me insistently. You say: do you realise, we are having our first debate? I say: perhaps the purpose of fathers is to bring their sons together. You say: I enjoy talking to you. Decidedly, meeting you was a significant event. How many times in the course of one's existence does one have the certainty that one has met someone who truly matters? This is how I feel about you. Ah, Vincent, if you would only accept, I believe we could be friends. I say: I am already your friend. The moment we spoke we were friends.

Tell me about your mother. They say she was the

great love of your life. Tell me of this thing which is something alien to me, something mysterious, something barely imaginable. In saying this, I feel certain that I will displease you, that I should not say such things, that you will despise me for them, though you might deny it. But I prefer to be honest with you, Marcel. You would despise me more if I were to pretend to be other than I am. Yes, Marcel, speak to me of a son's love for his mother, and the tenderness of a mother for her son. You say: it is difficult to speak of *Maman*, I mean to speak of her directly, to name her. My books speak of her: you shall have to read them.

Among other things, books serve to enable writers to speak of their mothers. Everything you could wish to know about mine you will find in my writings. She is everywhere. She is there at the beginning, in the first sentence that I write, she never leaves me. Her presence pervades everything. She is my protecting angel, my guide, she it is who shows me the way. My worship of her is religious. You cannot imagine the influence that she exercised over my life, and which she exercises still, almost ten years after she passed away. I often think that my life, my whole life, has been fashioned by my relationship to her, that everything proceeds from her. I ask: but did you never rebel? You reply: yes, naturally, rebellion and surrender are inseparable, as hate is never far from love. Understand me, I had, too, to live with the feeling that I was not exactly the son she might have wished for, this was something I had to accept, something with which I had to come to terms, despite my sense of guilt. I conceded nothing in essentials, besides, how could I? In the last years of her life, we fought. And the son always triumphs over the mother, that is the course of history, that is time's victory. I waited, longer perhaps than others, for time to offer me this victory. But, I tell you, as a son, I am inconsolable. My mother's death was my greatest tragedy. I was devastated. I thought I would not survive her death, that I would not have the strength. I say: but you did survive. You say: you say that with precisely the clarity of thought and expression that I sensed in you. But be careful, even so, not to hurt those who love you. I say: I did not intend to hurt you. I simply believe that we survive everything, that life triumphs over everything. I think time is an assassin which sweeps away the faces of the past and takes with them the sorrows which we feared we might never survive. You say: you do not love your mother, then? I say: you were not listening to me. I bear my mother no ill-will. I simply no longer feel any tenderness for her. She and I have learned to pretend, and to make do with pretence. You say: it is a sad life for a young man, though you may not realise it. I say: my life is not sad, Marcel; I have you.

You look at me, touched by the compliment I have made you. You are unsure whether or not to believe the compliment. You say nothing. You prefer not to know.

You prefer rather to believe that it is true and to keep the compliment as a tender keepsake. I follow your train of thought. I say nothing. Above all, I say nothing.

Eventually, you pick up the conversation. You know, I have no wish to be a replacement father to you. There is nothing of a father in my character. Nor is this the kind of relationship I wish to have with you. You understand why I do not wish to be a father and ask of you something other, do you not? Yes, of course I understand. I know that you will have no descendants, that no doubt you real-ised this early in life, that you accepted it, that you would not wish to be encumbered by a child, that fatherhood is something quite alien to you. This much was apparent from the first. It is hardly, therefore, something which I would seek in you. It is all the less likely that I should seek it since I do not feel that I lack a father figure, I feel no such disappointment, it is not a concept I feel I need to hold on to. I do not want you to be my father, Marcel. I have said this already and I will say it again; it is not a difficult confession for me to make: I want you to be my friend and I truly believe that this is possible; you must forget, as I have, the difference in our ages, our pasts and, above all, our futures. You must follow the logic of your desire for my company to its conclusion. You say: how do you do this? How can you intuit everything, understand everything, make everything appear so simple? And this candour of yours . . . I say: it is important to try and be as truthful as possible. It requires the least effort.

Strangely, the bustle of the café fades. It is as though modesty reasserts itself in these suddenly muted conversations. Beside us, a couple look at each other in silence. Further off, an old man is engrossed in *Le Figaro*. Outside, on the pavement, the men seem to be walking with exaggerated slowness. I take a moment to observe this lull. I look away. You ask: what are you thinking? I reply: precisely, nothing. I am watching this world around us, this singular world of café society, this world is a fleeting moment, a chance meeting. I don't think we shall again be in the company that we share at this moment, that those who are here now do not know one another, that they are here by pure coincidence and that they will disperse without the slightest sense of loss. They will not see one another again, this existence will last only the time it takes to drink a coffee, read a newspaper, write a letter, recount a childhood. It is an idea that appeals to me, though I could not say exactly why. You say: it is transience and chance which interest you. It is the present, its futility, its essential mortality, which interests you. That is what it means to be sixteen: to live always in ephemeral moments, whereas I love only those things which endure, whose roots are buried in the past, in memory. My life is behind me and I work to rediscover it, to reassemble it, to give it meaning. That is another difference between us. I say: you are right. The work you speak of is something I would not even think to attempt.

You say: at sixteen, we believe we have no memories, we believe we have only a future. On the whole, you are correct, absolutely correct, in that life is waiting for you, like a boulevard rolling out before you, like an uncharted path whose end is unknown. But you are wrong, absolutely wrong, in that it is possible that the crucial events have already been played out; that everything has been fashioned in childhood, in the years you have already traversed: what will happen may be only a consequence of what has already happened. That is why I work with memory. Some think of it as mere nostalgia, they say I am retrospective. I study the past the better to control the present and I discover feelings in the present which I know from experience of the past. Memory weaves a connection between yesterday and today. It is as simple as that. No need to look any further. I say: time is these moments I spend with you, it is no more than that.

A waiter appears discreetly and, with a conspiratorial air, passes you a message which he slides on to the table like a secret communiqué. I am amused by his performance. I find it comical that he should try to transfer your importance to the message and thence, by extension, to the messenger, that is, himself. You do not notice this faintly ludicrous manoeuvre. You affect indifference to the world about you and focus your attention entirely on the message. You say: may I? I excuse you with a nod. You read attentively as though your whole life depended on the contents of this message. You assume the look of concentration which one reserves for the most difficult writings. You look up: dear child, I am afraid that we shall have to bring our conversation to an end. The Marquise de V is very ill and is asking for me. Well brought up, I enquire: nothing serious, I hope? You say: the Marquise de V is on her deathbed so often that news of her demise will be greeted with the greatest scepticism. But her friendship is very important to me, as I believe mine is to her. So we have a duty to one another. I say: so you are leaving me? You say: yes, but we shall see each other again very soon. Next time, we will meet at the Ritz, it is my headquarters, you know. I say: there are worse places from which to do battle. You smile. As we part company, you say: what's this? Are you not going to kiss me today? Surely you are not intimidated by the crowd. This seems to be a challenge, though I believe that, in your heart, you do not think I will accept, nor do you wish me to. So I throw my arms around your neck. You stiffen a little in the face of this unexpected effusiveness. You struggle to maintain your composure, though you do not quite succeed. About us, no one has had the restraint not to turn to look. To murmurs and shocked looks, we leave the café.

Marcel, I love the heedlessness that you allow me.

7

I come to your body once more. I move from one world to another. It is not so difficult to do.

First, you take me in your arms. Your immediate, instinctive reaction is to touch me, to press against me, to impress your body on mine, to wait for the moment when they are in symbiosis, the moment when marriage makes them one flesh. First, you seek out my lips, you sketch out a kiss, you find my tongue, our saliva blends. First, there is this irresistible passion, this need for one another, for sensual intimacy. First, you are silent, you do not say a single word. The room is filled with our silence, filled with the sound of bodies brushing against each other, with the sighs of mingled mouths. It is the most sensual of silences, one which says all there is to know about who we are, what binds us, what our future holds. I leave everything to you. More than that, I expect you to behave like this. My mouth travels down the length of your chest, which I have bared. It tries in vain to possess the skin, the muscles, the bones, the very substance. It is a carnivore's kiss. Sometimes, I feel a shudder. I know that this is pleasure, that there is no guilt, no sense of wrong-doing, not in this moment in which we offer ourselves. My lips continue their descent, stop as they reach the lower abdomen, where the flesh is firmest, where its strength can be measured, where power resides and where, even so, it seems most vulnerable, where the risk is most evident because your defences are down. And, then, my mouth brushes lightly against your member. I am filled with wonder at the softness of your sex. I do not know, I cannot know, if all men are the same, but I have an inkling of the universal softness of the male sex. With my tongue, I slide back your foreskin. I know these acts of pleasure like an expert, like a novice. I know them as though I have known them for eternity, as though they were innate. Your sex hardens in my mouth. Nothing can stop us.

It is only as the semen dries on our tired bodies that you decide to speak. It is only after we have made this solemn communion that you feel able to say a word. And I know, of course, that you speak of the war, that you cannot do otherwise, that you cannot escape this obsession, this thing which weighs upon you until it has become you. You say: the great leveller in war – greater than conscription, greater than arriving in the alien land that is the front, greater than the first awkward words exchanged with your companions in adversity, those who share with you the chance of being dead tomorrow, greater than the feverish waiting, the freezing flows of mud, greater than the shouted orders – is that first time you leave your trench and go over the top. That precise moment, that first time, that truly is war, your own war, your greatest risk. Those bodies so exposed, that offering, that is the greatest risk. You have to have lived that moment to understand the absolute, utter, unconquerable terror, the madness, the suicide. Nobody else can understand. It is incomprehensible to any of you. And, strangely, I envy you that incomprehension, though it is not your fault that you cannot understand. I resent the living because they do not know what it is like to be dead, I resent those who stayed because they do not know what it is like to have gone, I resent the people who tell stories that they have not lived because they speak without knowing. And, in a way, that resentment is one of the things that helps me to hold out. I say: do you resent me, too? You say: I could never resent you, though you have been given everything, though you have been spared everything, even though you must be the person I should resent most of all. How could I resent you when I have loved you for so long?

I think: he has just spoken those words: I love you. He has just spoken that sentence: I love you. This thing he has said puts me in a state of exultant terror. I am incapable of the slightest movement. I keep my own counsel. He has stopped speaking. The resonance of this thing he has said hangs in the air. It fills the whole room. After a moment, I put my head on his stomach, my warm cheek against his firm flesh. I think: Arthur, we are living the greatest adventure that ever was.

My head against your stomach still, my eyes on the limp flesh of your sex, I hear you say: when you go over the top, you consent to die, but you want fervently, furiously, to live, and this fervent, furious desire to live can only be expressed by the death of another, of the enemy. War is a pendulum. I survive only if he dies. We win only if they die faster and in greater numbers than we do. It is as simple as that. So we go over the top to kill. Our bellies are churning with fear, but we go out to kill. Our bayonets offer ludicrous protection if they have the advantage of numbers, if they use shell or gas, but they are our only protection. We can depend on nothing else. We come to love our bayonets as though they were human, as though they kept us company. We hate them, too, when they jam, when they are nothing more than butcher's knives aimed blindly, tearing through meat, skewering anonymous bodies in a ghastly carnage. Vincent, I've killed men, German soldiers, lads my own age, who had the same blond hair, the same blue eyes. I'm sure some of them were handsome. I'm sure that, like us, some of them wanted nothing to do with all this. I don't know how many there were. I don't know how many of them died because I ran them through. One day, I stopped counting because it was a number too terrible to reckon. Vincent, you're sleeping with a murderer. I say: I am sleeping with a man who managed to stay alive, with a survivor. I am sleeping with you, Arthur, and it is amazing.

You say: forgive me for talking about death all the time, when we should be talking of nothing but love. You are forgiven. How could you do other than talk of death, which hems you in day after day? What is more, without it, without this threat to your life, would we ever have met? I curse the war, of course, but with the same gesture I bless it, because it is war which has given you to me, which has sent you rushing into my arms. You say: don't say that. I can't bear to hear you say it. Because you ask it, I will not say it again.

And so silence descends again upon the room which has been mine since I was a child. I stare at the shutters closed over the open window. I study the red border of the tapestry; the photographs on the wall; the copy of an El Greco; the furniture of a previous century, from the homes of ancestors long gone; the ornate mirror over the marble fireplace, the tattered armchair and the bed where we find ourselves lying among the tangle of family linen, that same linen which bears the monograms of my father and mother like some ludicrous coat of arms. I look at this tiny world which cannot measure up to us, this peculiar place in which I never imagined I would lose my virginity, this indeterminate space in which we pitch and roll deliciously. I think how strange life is, after all. I turn back towards you and I kiss your face; your eyes are closed.

You begin again: you can't imagine what it's like. Imagine two shattered armies face to face, forever launching a new offensive only to return exhausted and decimated. Picture it: the men at their wits' end sent to the front line to face troops who can no longer survive on patriotism alone. And the shortage of munitions, leaving us wanting, at the mercy of the enemy. And the succession of trenches in which each time we bury ourselves a little deeper in mud, always a little deeper. And the corpses mown down by machine guns, hanging lifeless on the barbed wire like human trophies, a measure of our victory or defeat. And the daily ritual of checking every body to make sure it is still alive, finding a neighbour dead. Every day we wake to find that we are fewer. Every day, I think of the cemeteries of white crosses across France, though I've never seen them, of bells tolling for the dead, the funeral marches, so slow and so heartbreaking, of the salutes fired under the cypresses in honour of the dead, of the speeches casually composed by local councillors, which will serve again at the next funeral; I think of the absent family, because we die so far from our families, because they could not identify the body which must be buried all the same. I think of these things and all the time the astonishment of being a survivor weighs me down.

I think, too, of the common graves, of the anonymous ossuaries, of the nameless corpses, their limbs confused in a final humiliation, the severed hand of one on the mutilated face of another and the earth over them, the earth which, in the end, covers everything, the earth under which our lost youth will moulder.

You say: we shouldn't talk about this any more, but it is impossible not to.

I say: I love your skin, your smell, the life that pulses within you. I listen to you, but all I want to remember is your skin, your smell, the life that pulses within you. I know that being here in your arms is the most important thing. I know that nothing is more powerful than this; that war and forgetfulness can do nothing to destroy it. Me, here, in the space between your arms. That first night with you was a birth, a coming into the world, a dazzling ray of light. Everything else: the suffering, the fear, I take upon myself. I am here, Arthur. All you need do is let go, let everything go. If you can let go – not much, just a little – it will all be different. You say: you're right. Something wonderful, something miraculous is happening to me; I am with you. That is all that matters.

When the room falls silent again, I think: this is our third night together. The third of seven nights which make up your leave. It is a week in the summer of 1916. I am sixteen, with black hair, green eyes. My name is Vincent de l'Étoile. This week has been exceptionally sunny. This has been a week of upheavals: the week in which I met Marcel P. and Arthur V., in which I encountered a mind and a body, in which I unexpectedly came face to face with the easy life and the possibility of death. I believe in chance, so much so that I would not wish to see in these two things more than coincidence. I try to find sleep and, at length, I do.

As day breaks, I study your face, turned from me and resting on your right arm; the folds at the nape of your neck; the hollow between your shoulder-blades where the sun has cast a pool of light; your back strewn with freckles, like points of reference for later use; your downy buttocks on whose crown the sheet has come to rest; your heavy sleep. This is an instant of you for ever, whatever might befall.

8

The Ritz, it transpires, has a shameless majesty, an astounding opulence which strikes one like an offence, an insult, and yet one accepts it as a delicacy, as a gift one feels one does not quite deserve. I move from Arthur's feverish embrace to the obsequious attentions of a servile concierge, from the sickness of war to the radiant health of the rich, from the serious to the futile, from the consciousness of the many to the frivolity of a few. For the first time I find the crossing from one side to the other difficult. At first you do not notice my unease, or, more exactly, you do not suspect it: why should you look for unease in a boy whom nothing seems to trouble. You say: I trust the place Vendôme has lived up to your expectations! You go on: what do you think of my palace? You know it is the most modern, the most luxurious in all of Paris? We have electricity on every floor. Ah, I tell you, Venice is the only place left in the world to rival Paris! Did you know that here you may chance upon a prince or an actress, not to mention an ageing writer? I reply: no, I didn't. In fact I know nothing. I know nothing of this life. At this you realise that something in my manner has changed. You ask: is there something worrying you that you would like to tell me about, dear child. I say: why do you call me 'your child'? I thought you did not wish me to call you 'Papa'. You narrow your eyes and say: well, Vincent, it would seem we are having our first quarrel. In saying this, of course, you turn the tables; you force me to beat a retreat if I do not wish to appear uncouth. I say: I apologise, Marcel. I didn't come here to cross swords with you. Quite the reverse, you know how much I enjoy your company, how much I delight in these afternoons which you are kind enough to afford me, in what have become our daily assignations. Perhaps I was a little taken aback by the grandeur of the place, when only a moment ago we saw German zeppelins fly over our heads. Perhaps it is a little surreal to meet you here when the shelling is getting ever closer. You say: though it may surprise you, one has an excellent view of the war from the windows at the Ritz. From here I contemplate a city brought to its knees, the most beautiful city in the world menaced with destruction. I watch the terrified populace of Paris, and remember, I know these people of old. Furthermore, I believe one can wage war by throwing concerts or giving supper parties. I truly believe so. One can fight the enemy with art. One can fight the enemy by going on with one's life. To cower and hide would be victory for them, and our unmitigated defeat. I will not hide out in a cave. That is simply not who I am. I will carry on receiving guests, listening to the divine Fauré being played, writing my books at night during the black-out. I shall thumb my nose at the Germans after my own fashion. This is the only way I can wage this war, I have nothing else. I am an artist, an asthmatic, a man of the world!

I am not asking you to account for yourself, Marcel. It is not in my nature. You have no need to justify yourself for something for which, in any case, I do not reproach you, because there is nothing to reproach. I did not intend to force you to speak of the war. It is, in fact, a road down which I prefer not to go, because I know that I know nothing of it. Being sixteen is my excuse. You say: it is, quite clearly, no excuse at all, but it is such a pretty one that we will gladly accept it. And you continue: I am neither a pacifist nor a warmonger. I think I should prefer to be indifferent to this war as to all wars. I would prefer that this war did not affect me, did not shape the way I live. I would have liked to stand apart. But of course, such a thing is impossible. This war affects all our lives. You know that my brother, Robert, is a doctor working in makeshift hospitals at the front, and the admiration and respect I feel for his dedication and his courage are as fierce as the dread that I feel each time a letter arrives, a letter which may bring me word of his death. And I too must live with my dead, must carry on when those I love have died there. I had a good friend, one dear to my heart, who fell in the first days of the fighting. I write about my dead. That is my subject, I have no other. In these times of blood and fury, I try to write something in which the dead take the principal roles. That is all I do. That, and dine at the Ritz during the air-raids. No doubt you find such things curious. It is just that I am inconsolable.

I say nothing. I have listened to your voice in the vast, menacing silence of the drawing room at the Ritz. I listened as your words filled this extraordinary space, echoed among the imposing mirrors, the red drapes, the gilded chandeliers. I watched as your words took over the space. Suddenly, there was nothing here but you, your sombre voice unfolding your war. And then, your final words, uttered like a heartbreak that encapsulated your whole life: it is just that I am inconsolable. I say nothing.

And then, after some time, I say: I did not imagine that my words would provoke such a response when I expressed, rather awkwardly, my discomfort at finding myself in this place, here, now. That discomfort has vanished, to be replaced by that of having offended you, of having misjudged you and reopened, perhaps, wounds that have never healed. You say: Vincent, you could never offend me. You are my angel, remember? And now it is you who kiss my hand. That is precisely what you do: you take my right hand, turn it slowly and look at it for a moment or two, then you lean forward, bend towards the palm of my hand and kiss it delicately. I feel your moist lips on my skin, the hairs of your moustache, your asthmatic breath. Around us, the silence seems to have become even heavier. The ballet of waiters and *maîtres d'hôtel* seems to have frozen momentarily. There is nothing but your face pressed into the palm of my hand. Your final words still ring in my head: I am inconsolable.

You start to speak again, and when I hear you, I am afraid. What you have said is sufficient unto itself, it requires nothing more. I am afraid that the power of your words will be diminished now if you say something of less consequence, that it will be lost through a pretentious desire to press your advantage. I fear this, and I do not want to listen. I want to stay in the cathedral silence of the great drawing room at the Ritz. You speak again: I was a soldier, once, a quarter of a century ago in Orléans. I did my military service there and, would you believe it, I enjoyed it? It was one of the happiest times of my life. One of the few in which I felt myself useful. One of the few, too, in which I could enjoy the company of young people who were not of the same upbringing and whose coarseness did little to mask their poetry, whose idleness made them no less disciplined, whose spontaneity quite simply captivated me. How can I explain it to you? There was an immediate, easy familiarity between us of the sort that one believes impossible among strangers, and that intimacy

gave me a sense of peace. This familiarity made everything easier. They were good people, these young men.
Now, I believe the men we are sending to be slaughtered
are the same, they have their frank, open faces, their
broad smiles, their muscular bodies, their clumsy gait,
their simple appetites. I believe that twenty-five years
on, it is the same story. It is the sons of my comrades
who are dying out there, though they wanted none of this.
I loved the army, Vincent, but I hate the war. I hate
this thing which has massacred a generation of simple
souls and trampled over my memories. Those happy
years, and they were few, perish under this hail of fire
and folly. Does one ever truly find peace, Vincent?

No. The answer, undoubtedly, is: no. No, Marcel,
you will not find peace. From time to time you will
allay some of your fears, some of your pain. At times
you will relive the rapture of those lost years. But you
cannot escape this slow death. You will suffer the
inescapable defeat which Time inflicts on all of us. All
is lost. From the very beginning, all is lost. No, Arthur,
you cannot escape the blight of war. Whether or not you
survive, you will be marked for ever by this war. With
me, you experience moments when you can distance
yourself from your pain, but they are no more than
fugitive moments. No, one never truly finds peace.

Yes. The answer, assuredly, is: yes. Marcel, you will
find peace somehow. Living with your dead, living in
the past; these are the things which give you the courage

to go on, to create a future, to be here still in spite of everything. Yes, Arthur, you can escape. If luck is on your side, you will come through, you will escape this carnage. And if you do, anything will be possible. Life will be beautiful. Mornings will be dazzling. Everything will begin again. Everything is perpetually beginning again. Yes, in the end, we all find peace.

I don't know. I don't know. How could I know?

9

By the fourth day, it has become like a ritual. Suddenly, I am spending every afternoon with Marcel, every night with Arthur. All of a sudden I move from one to the other like the sweep of a finely tuned pendulum. All of a sudden my whole life is organised, quite easily as it happens, around these two men. My habits have changed drastically and slowly I am becoming accustomed to new habits. I have not forgotten that the boundary for one of these habits will come at week's end, but I do not wish to think about such things. I want to experience only the moment, not the looming certainty that I will lose that moment, not the certain awareness that, ultimately, this moment must slip from present to past, only the joy of the moment and the graze of memory. But who would understand that?

I have scarcely returned from the Ritz when you tap at my window, like a secret lover (which is, after all, what you are). I clear a path for you and in a moment you are in my arms. I guide you to my bed and the communion of bodies begins. Making love, too, has become a ritual.

Something in your touch is more forceful than before, as though possession suddenly mattered to you, as though you felt forced to take the upper hand, as though this were an act of retribution for some evil spell cast on you. I consent to this aggression because I feel it is a necessary outlet. When at last you rest your tired body against my bruised flesh, when your chest and your stomach are pressed into my back, fused there by sweat, when our legs have interlocked like some self-regulating mechanism, I know that if I turned I would see terror in your eyes. You are a young man urged on by terror.

You say: these days are torture. I try to enjoy them to the full, to relish them, I know that they will be over soon, that I shall have to leave and that thought puts an end to all my pleasure. This week is just a reckoning, a countdown. I hate myself for thinking that, for saying that, but it is more or less the truth. The days I spend with Mother are terrible. They are like days from some future mourning when they could be simple, perhaps even happy. All possible gentleness is crushed in advance by the terrible frontier that is Sunday. Everything is cloaked in a terrible pain, in sorrow, in terrifying blackness. Mother cries. Often. I can tell that she is trying not to cry, but there is nothing she can do. She cries. And she asks me to forgive her for crying. At first I said, I forced myself to reply, to say: cry if you need to, it's all right; crying isn't so bad. I don't mind if you cry. Later, I said: these tears are pointless, they only make you suffer more. You must try not to be sad. Now, I say nothing. It's useless to speak. She cries into my silence, and, in the end, I take her in my arms. And so the days go by, she huddled against me. Besides, I think she cries so that she will not say things, terrible, dangerous, inexpressible things. It's a way of censoring herself, of mutilating herself so as not to make things worse. Because, of course, they could be worse. For her, talking would be worse. In the beginning I tried to steer the conversation to other things, but in the end everything we talked about, however tortuous the route, came back in the end to the proximity of death. The warning signs are everywhere. To talk of childhood seems to doom the future. One feels as though one is looking at photographs of a dead man. Talking about my father is impossible, forbidden. Even now, in our most intense, most intimate moments together, we cannot talk about my father. I don't press her. I resolve not to fight with my mother. Should I not make it home, I would not want her last memory to be a quarrel. That's it. The hours I spend with her are gruelling. And then there is you. You who have appeared out of necessity. You who are all my nights. You to whom I can talk, who listens. You who are sixteen, with your heady beauty. These nights with you are my salvation.

This room is a ship. A ship on which we plot a course over seas, sometimes calm, sometimes raging, searching for tranquil or rocky shores. We pass through fierce sun, and squalls of the sirocco. Sometimes the water stretches as far as the eye can see, and then, suddenly, a coastline. There is this constant rocking which can lull or shake us, but which is always there. We are sailors adrift on a drunken boat.

The journey goes on. You say: you will probably resent me for thinking of you as an adolescent, but that is what you are, and there is nothing shameful in that. Quite the reverse. It is a moment of indefinable grace, of beauty and poise. I want to tell you something, something I want you to believe: the love of a man for a woman cannot compare to the love of that same man for a youth. Love for a woman carries so many habits, beliefs, conventions in its wake that quickly it becomes something which, though pleasurable, is controlled, something which can no longer really surprise. Love for a youth encompasses every wonder, every fury; it has a desperate intensity; at every moment it is threatened with destruction, but it is lifted up by that very grace. A love like that has peaks and troughs, tremors and little deaths, dazzling light and terrifying shadows. All life is condensed into such an embrace.

I ask: is that all that you see in me, youth? You reply: I would like to say yes, it would be so much simpler. But the truth is something more. I can see beyond your youth. If my life is spared, I may ask you to share it with me.

I imagine I should say something, should not leave this declaration hanging, I should respond to this insane hope somehow, but how can I point the way? What could I say? I would rather be silent than wrong, than shatter this hope with some clumsy, faltering word, or feed it, knowing that in three days, perhaps three months, the war will take care of shattering it. Stay silent, and reserve my observations for the pages of a journal inked in private, in solitude. But why then do I write, when I could do nothing? Why this need to bear mute witness? Because this is the greatest of all adventures. Because life begins at sixteen and I am sixteen. Because Arthur's love is the most beautiful offering, the ultimate uproar. Because Marcel's friendship is a gift from heaven, something which should never have happened, whose chances of occurring were infinitesimal. Because this story is something exceptional. I, Vincent de l'Étoile, say: I am the lover of a soldier of twenty-one, I could be the friend of one of the greatest of living writers, these things inspire no shame, no glory, simply an immense, incomparable happiness. This moment of happiness is what I strive to capture in writing. Does one ever write other than to preserve a moment?

You say: I know very few people who are truly good listeners, who listen as you do. But listening should not prevent you from speaking. Why are you so silent? To this question, which I have answered in my heart, I respond again with silence. You close your eyes, bow your head, smile vaguely in resignation. I stroke the nape of your neck.

This movement of my hand to and fro on the nape of

your neck, stroking your short hair, is one of perfect intimacy, a timeless gesture of lovers. It takes us to a place where no one else can go. After a time, my hand slides to your chin; I lift your face; I want your eyes to look into mine, to feel the infinite tenderness of a gaze, locked one by another, to speak to one another without words. In your eyes I see at first a sort of sorrow, an absence. So I try to move forward, my gaze slipping inside you, effacing this sorrow, trying to bring back a flicker, a spark. And the transformation takes place, the flicker returns to your eyes, it comes from far off, and with it a smile which sketches itself upon your lips. There it is. Now we can be together once more. Your hand reaches towards my face, you run your fingers through my hair. I have won you back. Now we need only fall back on to the sheets.

For as long as I can, I will say nothing.

Your sleep is more than usually restless. Your body sweats on this July evening. It moves constantly, seeming to cross vast distances over uneven terrain. I see this body contort itself, this body which I have come to know so well. It is alarming to watch, though it is sensual too. You shudder again, more powerfully this time, and I decide to wake you. Your whole being oozes fear. Your eyes are panicked. I can see tremors of apprehension ripple on the surface of your skin. Your first instinct is to huddle into a ball. It takes almost a minute before you come to yourself. Then you say: what if we make it home, what if we make it out alive but disfigured, if our arms or legs have been blown off, our limbs have been amputated, if we have lost our sight, or the use of our arms, who will accept what is left of us, make the best of it. What about you, Vincent, would you want my disfigured body? I stare at you and, at length, I say: nothing will happen to you.

10

Another afternoon at the Ritz Hotel. This is your territory.

You begin by saying: I had a dreadful night, I couldn't write a single line. I had a terrible asthma attack. Asthma will be the death of me, you know.

Then, you launch into a detailed medical description of the asthma attack. I remember one phrase: the gasp of the dying. You tell me you have never been able to breathe normally, that you have suffered attacks since you were ten, that it is this which keeps you cloistered much of the time, that you must submit to interminable sessions of inhalation therapy. I listen to you whine like an old man for whom I would have no time whatever. I hate myself for thinking this. I should be more compassionate, more attentive to your ailments, but I cannot guess. I can guess what torture these attacks must be for you, what a cross an asthmatic has to bear. No doubt I am ill-disposed to listen to such complaints. I want to say: let us talk of something else, we can talk about your illness another time. I say nothing, of course.

After a time, you notice my inattention, or so I assume, because you say: it seems to me that there is something different about you, though I cannot say precisely what it is that has changed. Something in your manner, something in the quality of your silence, in the focus of your gaze. Everything leads me to believe that you are here, with me, but at the same time, you seem to be elsewhere, with another, perhaps. If I am mistaken, Vincent, please tell me so. I say: I assure you, you are mistaken.

There. I lie to you.

For the first time I lie to you, not by omission but by commission. And that childish affectation I have of 'assuring' you that I am not lying simply underscores the lie. In fact, I am almost certain that my face flushed crimson the moment I proffered the lie. I assure you, you are mistaken. How could such a thing escape a man whose judgement is so astute, whose powers of observation are renowned, whose ability to analyse each word, each gesture, has something of the surgeon about it? No, truthfully, I am not proud of this first lie. Or rather, I am not proud that I have failed to convince.

You say: I would be most disappointed to discover that you were concealing something of importance from me. I expect nothing less of my friends – and we are friends, are we not? – than that they be truthful and sincere in all circumstances. It is the very least one can expect of one's friends, for without that, what is friendship?

You have thrown down the gauntlet. You believe I have lied to you, but you are not completely certain. This threat to our friendship with which you blackmail me cuts me to the quick, it is your attempt to wrest a confession from me. The weight of guilt which you place upon my shoulders will, you hope, crush me such that I will be forced to recant, to confess my lie, to ask your forgiveness. I say: we share the same view of friendship, then. I, too, would be unhappy to think that you might have lied to me.

This is the solution I find, without even searching. I say this to you, without having planned to. In the first place I do not recant my lie. I do not even admit to it. I should doubtless not have lied, but now that the damage is done, I persevere. I feel that a confession would be worse than the lie itself. In the second place, I lessen the likelihood that it was a lie by indicating that I, too, consider sincerity to be one of the fundamental attributes of friendship. No one could say such a thing if he had lied only a moment before. Or if he did, he should be commended for his audacity. In short, I counter-attack. I, too, would not like to think that you could lie to me. Now the doubt is cast upon you. Suspicion passes from me to you. Does not this anodyne statement, said in the most detached tone, imply that, on occasion, you might not have told me the whole truth, the unvarnished truth? I have no idea whether you have ever lied to me. You may have, perhaps, turned things to your own advantage from time to time, as one naturally does in any attempted seduction. Whatever the case, a lie does not have the same seriousness for me as it would appear to have for you. I am sixteen. Nothing is truly serious to me, except death.

And, of course, my response finds its mark. You say: do you truly think I could have lied to you, Vincent? I should be very distressed if you were to think so. There! Already you are apologising, you are attempting to justify yourself for an offence of which, manifestly, you are innocent. I watch as you make the attempt. I adopt my most gentle, my most understanding air, while inside I cry victory! And then, I deliver the *coup de grâce*. I say: I don't believe for a moment that you could have lied to me. I know the value of our friendship. What is more, I could not bring myself to hurt you for the world. Marcel, the bond between us is the most precious thing in the world to me.

You are floating in the air of the drawing room of the Ritz.

When at last you come down to earth, it is to apologise once again and to say: Vincent, it is important that you should know that I have a faintly – or should I say utterly – dictatorial and possessive concept of friendship. I make many demands, often arduous demands, of my friends, though I am naturally happy that they should also make such demands of me. There is something else for which I must apologise in advance since

I know it to be unhealthy. I have a feeling, which to me is indivisible from the keen pleasure of friendship, a feeling which I cannot overcome, for one never truly prevails over one's nature, a passionate feeling of ownership. Though I wish it were not so, I habitually behave as though my friends were my private property and, in turn, I am at their disposal at any time.

Now I know exactly why I lied to you. And I remember your precise words: everything leads me to believe that you are here, with me, but at the same time, you seem to be elsewhere, with another, perhaps. It is this 'with another, perhaps' which is insufferable. In the first place, 'with another, perhaps' is false. No, Marcel, I am not with another when I am with you. In the second, I owe you nothing, by which I mean: I do not feel obliged to account for my actions to you. Our friendship is of great importance to me, but it too has its boundaries. I have my territories. To speak plainly, yes, this 'other, perhaps' does exist, and had I spoken to you of him it would have sparked an unforgettable jealous rage which I would have found difficult to stomach, because I cannot abide jealousy and because, simply, people are not interchangeable. There, Marcel, this is what I would like to say to you, and which I do not say.

Later, again on the subject of friendship, I hazard: do you enjoy similar relationships with women as with men? You barely pause before replying: why do you ask questions to which you know the answers? I interrupt as you are about to continue: because I would like to hear you speak of the difference.

You say: the friendship that I feel for women is that which, as an adolescent, I felt for the mothers of my friends; it has remained so through all these years. I like the temperament of women, Vincent. I like their temperament above all else. And, of course, I admire their elegance. To be a woman is to be charming, otherwise she might as well not be. What more do you want? Do you wish me to say I prefer women who are older than I? It is perfectly true. And, following your finely honed train of thought I will confess, besides, that I find their motherly charm suits me. I love the mother within the woman, that is to say, I like to feel like a son. In this way one may be in love and yet feel no desire. A woman inspires reverence in me, I wish to seduce her, to be near her, to be her confidant. I am not a lover, and never have been. But, truly, I am one who is in love.

This phrase lingers: I am not a lover, and never have been. I wonder how this regret manifests itself? I do not ask.

I say: but you have said nothing whatever about men! You exclaim: ah, men! There are two categories of men: those whom one admires, they are the fathers, the illustrious, the wise, the noble; and there are those whom one courts; they are the young, the gifted, the idle, the frivolous. There are delicious young men, you know? With beautiful green eyes. They are preferable to obtuse or dissolute women. And of course one may remain pure while loving young men, no? I do not answer what appears to be an assertion rather than a question, though I am unsure whether you mean that one must love young men in order to remain pure, or that one may remain pure in spite of loving young men. Before I have completed this thought you deliver this incomparable phrase: young men are, in the end, a pretty consolation.

At this, I think of what you have said: I am inconsolable. This, then, is what consoles you: young men.

I ask you: is that what I am, a consolation? At this, you jib: my dear Vincent, my good friend, even if it were no more than that you should not be offended, for, to my mind, that is a very great compliment! Yes, Vincent, you are a consolation to me for my life. But there is something other, too, something touching desire, the everlasting conflagration of desire.

Silence again. Heavy, full.

Then you speak: I am much taken by your intelligence, this manner you have of looking at the world without judgement, perhaps without morality, your comparative indifference, your youth. My own youth is so remote. How difficult it was for me, then, to be loved. One of my lifelong regrets is that I was not beautiful, and what is more, that I turned for love to those who could not but reject me.

'Could not but reject me', not 'could not love me in return'. I remember the force of the phrase. And suddenly,

I can almost see him, this young Marcel, Marcel at sixteen, not quite handsome, too heavy-lidded, too swarthy in appearance, this Marcel who craves a little love, too much love, from those who cannot give him the love he needs and who, sooner or later, reject him, who say to him: no, we want nothing to do with this love, and young Marcel presumed they meant 'we want nothing to do with you'. He was as old as I am now, he is terribly alone, he is alone still. Thirty years have passed.

11

At the foot of the great marble staircase, my father contemplates the portrait which D painted of him. I am struck by this mirror image of excess and by the vanity of this man who had to have his portrait painted purely to flatter his ego. My father, of course, insisted that it was a legacy, that he had a moral obligation to generations to come, that for centuries, every member of our family has had his portrait painted. I think he is capable of believing his own foolishness, and I am well aware that he attaches great importance to our lineage, as though we were thoroughbreds entrusted with propagating the species. It must be said that my sisters have taken to this task with a zeal which warrants admiration; seven heirs between them in less than five years! I am afraid, dear father, that I may be unable to demonstrate such prowess. The survival of the species is of little interest to me and – dare I confess it? – I even dream sometimes of the collapse of empires.

He interrupts his contemplation only to deliver one of his endless harangues. He is, needless to say, 'extremely proud' of the affection in which I am held by our 'eminent man of letters, he will be a member of the *Academie* one day, mark my words', but 'all the same', is it not a little ostentatious, 'while the fighting rages' (does it ever do otherwise?), to be seen every day at the Ritz? Our 'patriotism, much-admired by everyone' (what have we ever done to demonstrate this virtue?) could be cheapened by small-minded prattlers who might read into my flagrant public appearances at the grandest of Parisian hotels with a man partial to society gatherings some disrespect for 'our valiant soldiers in combat'. This verbiage, to which I should, I suppose, have become inured, never fails to disconcert me. I brace myself to say nothing and to escape to my room to wait for Arthur at precisely that moment that the scope of his rant widens to include my own 'valiant soldier'. At this point I know what is coming, I know it by heart, the class system is about to make a spectacular come-back: My boy, I've already told you how much I disapprove of such relationships. Yet it has been brought to my attention (who are these people who seem to have nothing else to do but to bring to the attention of parents the turpitudes of their progeny?) that you have been spending time with that young man, Blanche's son. (I tremble a little, as what time I spend with Arthur is between my sheets.) I'm told you were seen talking to him from your bedroom window. (I can never thank these spies enough for their incompetence.) I do not deny it. What good would it do? The scolding continues: and you just stand there and say nothing. Dear boy, whatever are we going to do with you? And with that, which is my father's most severe admonition, he turns on his heel to signal his displeasure. Dismayed by this pathetic and ineffectual display of parental authority, I take the marble stairs four at a time. When I reach the top, I turn for a moment. In my turn I gaze at the portrait of my father and I determine that no such likeness will ever be made of me. Surely it is important to leave no trace behind?

When you come to me, I relate the incident, taking care to skip over the part concerning Marcel, expecting nothing more than a smile and your support, but in a weary voice tinged with despair you say: at least you have a father you cannot talk to.

Then, though I have not asked, you tell me of the father you never knew, hence *de facto* absent, and of the wound left by that absence. A gaping void that nothing can ever begin to fill. The certainty of disappointment, like some infirmity, some monstrous, almost shameful handicap dragging pain and suffering in its wake. You tell me of the feat of imagination it takes to try and fashion an image of this father, and the devastation and despair that follows each inevitably vain attempt, each effort doomed to failure.

You tell me of your birth certificate, which bears only your mother's name, the shame your mother felt to be forever dismissed as an 'unmarried mother'. You tell

me of the disgrace which she bears as one bears a burden, or a blame; the mockery, the whispered insults
behind her back, the condemnation of those who profess
to be good merely because they are steeped in religion.

You tell me of this skewed lineage.

You say: sometimes, I would rather a dead father
than no father at all. No, not sometimes, you add, often.

You tell me of your childhood, when you were jeered
at school, when you were forced to invent stories of a
father who was an adventurer, a traveller, who was missing or dead in some unspecified but perilous conflict,
and when the lies found you out, you were pointed at,
laughed at. You say: children wound most deeply when
they are cruel, their aim is perfect, and the memory of
the pain lasts longer. I still remember the laughter, the
sarcastic remarks.

You speak to me of a mother who tells her son nothing despite his pleas, a mother who creates a wall of
silence about her, who prefers the hatred of her child to
the pain of confession. You say: I remember the cries,
the tears.

You say: becoming a schoolmaster is a means of
becoming part of society, of being accepted in the world,
no longer being an orphan. At the École Normale des
Instituteurs, at least, the Republic did not ask me to give
an account of myself. You go on: I am not confused. I
know my pupils are not my children, but I believe they
will be a kind of family. I believe one can decide to

create one's own family beyond the ties of flesh and blood, an ever-changing family of new people, passing faces, smiles which have left their mark on one's memory. Conversely, I already know I will never have a child myself, in fact, I know that I shall never have the chance, it would be impossible. As an adolescent, I was not frightened or saddened by this realisation, by this discovery that I prefer the bodies of men to those of women, that I should never worship the body of a woman, that I would have no heirs. I accepted that my sexuality would console me for my childlessness.

I think: sperm rather than blood.

You say: I am a man without ancestors, without siblings, without descendants. I am of this world, but with no ties to this world. I am someone who does not know where he comes from, who has no one with whom to share his journey, who will leave no trace behind. When I die, my name will not be all that dies with me, my whole existence will be obliterated, consigned to oblivion. No one will remember me. You say: Vincent, will you be the one who will remember me?

I say: you are alive, today. I cannot talk about you in the past tense, I cannot think of you in the past, I do not know how to answer your question. You insist: it doesn't matter when I die, whether tomorrow or decades from now – you can be the one who remembers me, can't you? I think: whatever may happen, there are things which will endure, moments of passion, the force of your embrace, your breath on the nape of my neck, your silences and your words. The looks between us. I say: if, one day, we can no longer see one another, I will remember your face absolutely and precisely.

You say: at least you've said something, broken your usual silence. And, as always, when you break your silence it is to say something beautiful. Why don't you talk more often? There are things I need you to say, things that will reassure me, move me, keep me warm through the winters I have to endure in the midst of this summer. But you say nothing, or so little. Why do you let nothing slip, even if it were an accident, or a lie, some compromise you have made with the truth? I look at you and, as always when you hope for a word from me, I say nothing. I sit motionless in the heavy, ample silence. You look deeply into me, as though to extract from me this declaration for which you long, but your eyes meet my own which refuse to run this risk. After some seconds, no doubt a short time, though it seems long, you close your eyes, drop your head towards the sheets in a gesture of resignation. It is a scene we have lived already, which has become almost familiar.

I do not blame myself for my silence. I feel no guilt. I know the pain this silence causes you, I know that I should spare you this in these moments in which you can legitimately call upon my sympathy, but I know too, a notion ill thought out but certain, that it is better not to speak. In any case, what would I say? I contemplate your face which is turned away from me. And then, as I always do, I place my hand on the nape of your neck. I make this gesture, placing my hand on the nape of your neck, a gesture which only lovers can make, a mark of the fiercest intimacy. We linger like this, you, head down; I with my hand on your neck. I feel the softness of your close-cropped hair, the warmth of my palm against your skin. It is as though in this special touch of skin on skin I have found some certainty. A little later we are rolling in the tangled sheets. The silence is broken only by moans and gasps, by the breathlessness of exertion and the cries of release.

When at last our sweaty bodies are still, like burning corpses, I reformulate this promise to myself: for as long as I can, I will not speak.

I take this vow of silence, so that everything can remain in this state of absolute purity, of complete whiteness. My words are destined only for the school copybook in which I scribble in secret like a lovesick girl. My words are destined only to record something of what has happened, some witness to what is. I answer Arthur's prayer after my fashion: I save our lives from oblivion.

Does one ever tell a tale other than one's own?

12

We are in your room, your territory once more. I have come to you here, here where you spend most of your feverish days and nights. You say: come in, Vincent, don't be afraid. Do you realise that it is here, between these cork-lined walls, in this shadowy, confined space, its windows almost perpetually closed, that the essential takes place? Do you know that it is here that I create?

You have never asked me about my book, you have never felt the need to do so; perhaps that would be very much in character. I look at you, at your lovely indifference, your remoteness from the world, from men, and I think, decidedly, here is someone cut from a very different cloth from the people I frequent or even from those I see only occasionally. In the main, they see nothing more in me than the great writer and immediately they cannot but ask about the mysteries of the writer's art, the agony of creation, before the conversation rolls inevitably on to the trappings of fame. At the outset, they try, with some sincerity, or with none, to understand. They profess their fascination for this strange occupation that is a writer's. That is all: they hurl this fascination in your face and leave you to make of it what you will. They think of it as a gift, as the paying of homage, when in truth it is simply proof of an ignorance of which none can ever cure them. And then they move on to fame, which is the one thing which truly interests them, the one thing which has prompted them to speak to you, though they would never admit as much. They hope that in touching gold, some little lustre will rub off on their skin, skin which absorbs nothing. It is a bizarre comedy in which vanity mingles with something akin to a child's wish. I do not really know whether to be touched or saddened by it. And you, of course, you are not like this, Vincent. You do not talk of my books or my notoriety. You seem almost to be unaware of them. Nor is this an affectation, some pose that you have chosen to assume. This is how you are, is it not? Indifferent. Consequently, it is with you more than with anyone that I wish to talk about my writing. I wish to answer the questions you do not ask. It is in deference to your absolute purity, to your almost virginal honesty, that I wish to bear witness. And even if you say nothing, I know at least that you will listen. Better, I know that you will understand.

Writing requires complete commitment. One may do but one thing: write. One must not allow oneself to be distracted. One must dedicate oneself completely to the book, sacrifice everything else. It is a vocation, it is a religion into which one is initiated. Do you realise that, even when I am not writing, I am writing nevertheless? Time spent in contemplation, in observation, in society, in idleness, all of these contribute to the task of writing. When it appears that I am indolent, a vice for which I am often reproached, I am, in truth, working on a book. I live only to write. It is impossible to do otherwise. And this hunger becomes more acute when, as I do, one senses the end of one's life fast approaching. I must finish those books to which I have dedicated my life. You must understand that nothing is more important to me than to finish those books. I hope that I shall be granted sufficient time. I write in haste, in tumult, in terror. You may think that I am prey to some unwholesome passion, and you would be correct.

Writing is the meaning I give to my existence. My existence vanishes behind what I write. Or I might say: if I did not write, I truly believe I would be dead.

Your words resonate in the foul air of this asthmatic's room, this cramped, oppressive atmosphere crushed by its narrowness: if I did not write, I truly believe I would be dead. And I believe that you struggle to survive, to save your skin in this improbable space, this fury of composition. I find the idea both wretched and wonderful, pathetic and magnificent. I feel a tender pity for you and an intense admiration.

You continue: writing is a labour. Doubtless talent has some small part to play in the business, but, above all, one must work, and work flat out, one must instil discipline in oneself, rules, effort. And so, when night falls, as you will have deduced, I sit at my desk and I write. I write until I am exhausted, I write until I have conquered insomnia or until my hand fails. You cannot imagine how painful it is when the hand constricts and will write no more, when the arm becomes so taut, so stiff that one must put down one's pen. When, much as one wishes to continue, one cannot write more. It has become physically impossible to write, to make the slightest movement. It is enormously frustrating. At such moments, I calculate precisely the time wasted. When it becomes unbearable, I waken Céleste and ask her to write at my dictation. You should see these hours of reckless enterprise, it is quite indescribable. It is a scene such as one sees only in the theatre.

Of course, I realise that one must not force oneself to write when one is not disposed to do so. One must wait for it to come, for it to happen. Equally, the act of writing should not be overly prolonged; when one feels that it is finished, then it is finished. One must not be stubborn. And yet I am stubborn. I attack my writing. I force it to come. I coerce it into being. I ceaselessly put off the moment when I must set down my pen. As I have said before, only exhaustion can halt my flow.

Sometimes, when one has finished a page, one feels as though one will never write another, that the book will come to nothing, that it will never be born, that one will be unmasked and this colossal masquerade will be exposed for what it is. At such times one feels wretched, desolate. And then, it floods back. Without one necessarily understanding why, it returns. One can begin again, again to embark on the almost indescribable happiness that is writing.

You have no idea of the obstacles which one must overcome, the challenges one must accept, the resistance one must quell, not least in oneself, and the madness which all of this represents. It is truly an extraordinary achievement. It is an act of incredible courage and self-sacrifice. It can be a thankless occupation, which one would not wish upon one's worst enemy. There is much suffering in a writer's work. One endures such suffering. Those who consider me to be an idler, a good-for-nothing, a dilettante, should see the boundless energy I expend, the forces I marshal, the sheer effort of will which I deploy. They would not believe their eyes.

I am building a church. That is what I am doing. I am erecting a monument. The foundations of this are my childhood. A lifetime of things seen and intuited, of public events and personal adventures, have furnished the material for the walls. And in this church the story of men and women is told, in this church one communes with the same fervour, one comes within reach of the universal.

Or I might equally say: I am constructing a house. This work is a house whose rooms interconnect in the most skilful manner. See, the rooms in which we are born, in which we grow under the watchful eyes of our parents, in which we reinvent the secret language of lovers, in which, sometimes, we agonise and die. See the alcoves in which secrets are shared, intrigues are contrived, silence is broken. See the salons where the world is on display, where women dissemble, where elderly writers meet young men who are far from shy. It is a panorama in which, no doubt, some will recognise themselves.

The composition of a novel follows the same paths as the devising of a friendship. At first, one lies in wait, searching for he or she who might be a companion. One surveys the throng, and suddenly one's gaze comes to rest on one's prey, recognising in this gesture, that tilt of the head, something which one anticipates will in time become familiar. Then, and only then, one draws near, prepared now to seduce, eager to carry off the other's affection at the first attempt. One swiftly knows whether or not one will succeed, whether an attachment is likely. If so, there follows the agitation, the fear of defeat, the hope of victory, the rapture of shared smiles. The path may be tortuous and rutted, but it leads, even so, to the sea. In the tentative *rapprochement* that I have made with you, Vincent, I find the same troubles, the same joys as I do in writing a book.

The book is a child, too. First, one must be in love, or have been so; one must feel the fire of passion or the bitter sting of loneliness, the hollowness of absence, in order to begin a book. Love and writing are intimately linked, for one engenders the other. Only then may fertilisation take place, the mysterious journey of the vital seed, the fluid mechanics. Then comes the phase when one must carry the book, allow it to grow, take shape inside oneself, until at last it resembles something which, one day, might have a life apart. Such a thing takes time and patience. It has taken me forty years. One day, one knows the time has come to give birth to this child. At last one is ready to write the first sentence, to lay down on paper that first sentence which one has turned over in one's mind a hundred times. There is great pain, by which I mean physical suffering, in this birth, but there is also a deliverance. There are cries and tears where joy mingles with fatigue. Thereafter, the child begins to grow. One helps him, guides him. Of course, he falters, stumbles many times, but always he moves forward. The day will come when the book can survive without its author. One day, the book is there, solid, tangible; you see it cradled in hands that are not your own. It is then, Vincent, that you realise that it no longer belongs to you alone, or perhaps at all; it belongs to others, to everyone, to anyone who cares to offer an opinion, as though a parent welcomed the censure of others in the education of his child. At that moment, it is ended. One must accept this leave-taking. More than this, one must accept that the book will outlive its author, that it will survive after we are dead, that it will speak to people who know nothing of us, of who we were. Such paternity is a *via dolorosa*, but at the end of the path a light may shine.

Writing takes time. Please excuse me for saying it in so prosaic a fashion, but it is only in this way that I can get close to the truth: *writing takes time.* These thousands of pages chart the story of my life. The manuscript is enormous. It is slow work. Sometimes, it is difficult to find my own way, to remember all the twists of fate, the destinies that cross, the affairs that interweave, this world that writes itself. Céleste curses me, tries always to introduce order into this chaos. But you must not think that I am repeating myself, it would be impossible for me to condense it any further, I would be incapable of removing a single sentence without striking at the foundations of the whole. The story divides, comes together once more, it dares to attempt to fashion a whole from the minutiae of a life, each private and public incident. It is a tracery of sentiment and emotion.

Some will say that what I have written is unreadable, abstruse, incomprehensible, monotonous or I don't know what else. I have never denied that the book is difficult, and I have the greatest admiration for Gaston Gallimard, who encouraged me to leave my previous publisher, Grasset, and come to him so that he might publish the book as soon as this war ends, if some day this war ends. So, at present, I am in the throes of finalising this transition to a new publisher in a setting of elegance and serenity. After all, it seems preferable to have my work published by someone who truly loves my books, rather than someone who, from his remote exile, seems little concerned with me, don't you agree?

I make no response to this question, which can have only one answer. I watch you and, suddenly, for the first time, I realise that you are a personage, a personality and a person all at once. I persist in making the distinction between the great writer, the flamboyant socialite and the friend dear to my heart, but I accept that such distinctions are no doubt artificial, that you are all of these things at once, and that to attempt to unravel them is futile.

At last, a question wells up from nowhere, the only question I can imagine asking, the only one to which I have not deduced the answer from everything you have said: for whom do you write? You say: one writes for only a few. I write for my dead.

Later, you say: I have not been truthful, Vincent. I write for the living, too. I write for you, of course.

When we part, I savour the tenderness of our embrace.

13

This is the last night, this night which we never dared imagine, this night which carries within it the elemental sorrow of imminent separation, this night of which we have never spoken, this night which we cannot spend as we might any other, this night which it would be better to blot out if we could to shield ourselves from danger, this night which is almost beyond words. Tomorrow, you rejoin your battalion at Verdun. Tomorrow brings the misery of Verdun.

And before this last night, there was a last day, a last day spent with your mother. A day crippled by sadness, regret, stupor, measured out in tears and silence, its hours chiming out with desperate slowness, like the countdown to an execution. A day in which death has been on every mind, though it would be unbearable, unwelcome, to name it. A day of mourning before death. A day of impenetrable greyness.

You say: it is an ordeal I never thought I should have to face, it is unimaginable, an ordeal which only war or plague could bring about, I think. It is a pain so intense that it is impossible to sound its depth, its power, until it has passed. It is like walking over embers, kissing a razor's edge, it is like some rite of initiation swathed in blood and suffering. It is an unbearable separation, worse than an injustice, worse even than suicide. It rips away the last link with my own life.

You should have seen Mother's face, like the Madonna in religious paintings, her skin waxen, as though the years had conspired to wither, to destroy it. You should have seen the blank eyes, turned to heaven as though waiting for a sign, the contorted mouth, from which no sound comes because it has become impossible to scream, to speak. You should have seen the panicked hands, the body slipping out of her control, shaken by spasms, wracked with astonishing violence. You should have seen the pendulum swing between hysteria and hope-lessness, between struggle and acceptance, continually beginning anew, to be crushed anew, this struggle against some nameless thing which fills her every thought. And there I am, and can do nothing. I am a spectator to her distress. I know there is nothing to be done. Nothing.

Taking leave of my mother is first and foremost a physical act. Arms must give up their embrace of the other's body, hands must uncouple, the touch of skin on skin must end, eyes must free themselves from the other's gaze. One must withdraw, and as one with-draws, everything crumbles, as though one can live only through the other, as though one cannot live without the other.

It is a physical loss, a life fading, something bleeding away, a force that cannot be contained.

Then tears brim on your lashes. I see them pearl there among the blond hairs like grain. I wait for them to roll down your cheeks, for them to overrun, to fall on to your face, but you hold them back. Silence descends, your eyes turn away, looking at nothing in particular. This moment is never ending, this moment when the tears hang suspended on your lashes.

When you come to yourself again, it is to come to us.

You say: whether it is terrible or wonderful it will be unforgettable. How many moments in a man's life are unforgettable? And how many does he know in advance will be so? What we have to live through is momentous. What we have to live through is our story.

Should we make love as though for the last time, because it could be the last time, with an energy fired by despair and an ardent desire to be together in the happiness of this communion of bodies? I say: we should always make love as though for the first time, with the nervous passion of those who have never known this moment, and the unashamed good fortune of novices.

But how can you recapture the innocence of the beginning, the breathtaking passion of those first hours, that lost virginity? How can you forget a gesture now familiar, a body you have come to know? I say: simply allow yourself to be surprised, puzzled, amazed, and strive to surprise the other, still. It is possible, it is vital. Habit masks a fatal sting.

You say: but how can you forget that we may never hold each other again? I say: simply live in this moment, nothing else, and it is easy. One does not make love, you do not think about the next time. It is an act complete unto itself, which comes from nothing and from which nothing comes. It is an event, a fact.

You say: when I listen to you, everything seems so simple, and yet I know that it is not, that it cannot be so. I say: we are the ones who decide, we alone. You have the power to decide that things are simple.

You say: how can you be so certain, so resolute? How can you know such things, when you have never been with anyone before me? I say: sensuality is a form of knowledge. Though I never asked for it, it seems that I possess that intelligence. I have learned nothing and yet I know everything. I weigh up the apparent immodesty of what I have said and discover it to be precisely that: apparent.

You say: I need to tell you that with you I could forget the war a little. This at least, this thing which I never thought possible: to forget the war for a moment, to put this monstrous obsession in parentheses.

At first the images blurred, they were less to the fore in my mind, then they faded to the far corners of my memory and, suddenly, I had to make an effort to recall them. The nightmares have not been so bad. I have managed to find some peace for a while, some calm. I had forgotten the flavour of peace.

I want to thank you for this love, this tenderness. This tenderness I dared not hope for. In life, do we ever seek anything more than a warm shoulder on which to nuzzle, a chest to welcome one's head, a stomach on which to place a kiss? In life, do we ever seek more than these moments when we can let our defences fall, when blood pounds in our temples, when hair sticks to the nape of our necks, when the skin trembles, when we are at our most vulnerable?

It is a night filled with our silences, too. Silences are a rhythm, a breath. They give meaning to what is said. At times, they make it possible to endure the terrible violence of what is said. They make it possible to go on speaking. They are the moment when our eyes meet. Within them we find our pain and our remission, our grief and our redemption. They are religious silences, by which I mean silences like those which resound in churches. We have the fervour and solemnity of communicants.

Of course, these moments should not be too grave. Everything should remain simple. But it could be simple only if we were spirits, and we cannot make ourselves incorporeal. This night is incarnate, in that it is the symbol, the essence of the flesh.

Sometimes, hands become panicked, mouths fret as they find each other with difficulty, bodies tense at some awkward gesture. Sometimes, instead of floating, we sink and it seems as though we are clinging together like survivors of a shipwreck. And then, everything rushes back into place, bodies fuse, we are comforted. But I think: I must remember the awkwardness, too, the botched gestures, the abruptness, the missed beats, because these too are signs of love.

As the day breaks, you say: what will you do when I am not here? I do not know, I haven't thought about it, there will be time enough to find an answer to that question. I live in the moment, I do not want to regret not having made the most of our time. I put our separation completely out of my mind, I act as though it will never happen, right up until the last moment. I side with life, without a second thought, to the end, I do not steel myself against death, I do not grieve before it is time.

You say: I don't have your detachment, I can't forget that this is a farewell. It is like a weight crushing me.

You say: I need to know that you will think of me. Though it may be stupid, childish, perhaps even wrong, I need you to swear that you will. Only the knowledge that you will think of me can give me the will to go on living. I could answer you with words, I could say: yes, of course I will think of you, but I have already answered you with my actions, with my deeds.

It would be impossible not to think of you, it is something which I cannot even conceive. You have come into my life and become the centre of it, you wrought this spectacular change, this magnificent devastation, nothing will ever be the same; even now, nothing is the same.

You say: you will be my every thought. You will be the one who is there by my side, even at the risk of madness. I would prefer, by far, such madness to the daily barbarism, the colossal butchery that is waiting for me. I need to remember you so I can cope with whatever present is granted me. You say: I will remember you with these words: sixteen, black hair, green eyes. I hear you say these words which are my words, which I have always kept to myself, which I have spoken only when I am alone, or in my journal. I hear you say this: sixteen, black hair, green eyes, and at this I can measure the precise extent of our intimacy, the vast terrain of our shared thought. I realise that this is what it means to be lovers: using the same words to speak of the same things though one has never heard the other use them; these random similarities, this remarkable intimacy.

You are right. That is the first thing you must remember about me. I am sixteen, black hair, green eyes. Because that is what I am, what comes closest to encompassing me. He who speaks of me thus, speaks best of me.

At the moment we part, we choose not words, but silence. Only an embrace, a look. No kiss, no goodbye. Only your body departing while mine remains. Only the quickening beat of your heart, the slowing of mine. Only fear. Only time behind us and time before us. Only tenderness falling apart.

When the door closes, I realise that something else is beginning, something I do not recognise, where love fills every space but the object of that love is no longer there. I try to catch my breath. I do not cry. I do not cry.

This story is that of Arthur Valès and Vincent de l'Étoile. This is the story I am telling. If, one day, someone finds my notebooks, he should not question what is written, for everything I have said is true; he should feel no shame, for we feel no shame; he should make our names known to posterity rather than follow his impulse to conceal them from prying eyes; he should know that this is a story of love, not some fleeting rapture, for we know what we are doing. This story is that of Arthur Valès and Vincent de l'Étoile. This is the story I tell.

BOOK TWO

SEPARATION

Arthur,

It is less than an hour since you went, since you left this room, and your absence weighs on me like a death.

It is as though I have suddenly realised what is happening, as though I had only just realised that you are not here, that you will not be here. I look out over a vast, ruined landscape.

It is almost unreal. Unreal not to have known before how things would be after. Incredible to find myself so surprised. Surprised, dazed, crushed. Sadness, worse than ever.

I walk through the empty room made larger by your absence, so large it almost seems unbalanced. It is as though I have lost my bearings. Like walking in darkness, leaping into the unknown.

It is a mourning I will have to bear, because what I have to face is a death. I know you are alive. I pray that you will remain so. But I know, too, that you are unreachable, that where you are I cannot go, and I have no idea when the day will come when you will return.

I do not know how to fight this madness. I do not know how one comes through a trial such as this. I do not know anything at all. Your loss is my loss.

I do not know how to go on. But still, life must go on.

(letter unfinished, unsent)

My Friend,

I have had to leave precipitately for Illiers, where I have been summoned to settle some family business, the details of which I will spare you, as I know that you have no interest in such things, and in this, as in many other things, I cannot but approve of your sentiments.

It is the haste with which I left which compels me, though barely arrived here, to write you these few words so that you will not think that your dear old friend – if you will allow me to describe myself thus – has behaved towards you in a cavalier fashion, since when we saw one another the day before yesterday I made no mention of any such expedition. But, as you will understand, I did not know, at that time, that I would be called upon to make this journey without delay.

Forgive me if my account seems a little vague, or if I seem too much intent on justifying my actions to you, but I hold your affection so dear that I would not wish by some tactless act to jeopardise it.

Furthermore, I have, unsurprisingly, grown so accustomed to our daily assignations that being unable to see you saddens me to a degree that you could scarcely imagine. Ah, Vincent, you have succeeded so perfectly in finding a place in my heart that some few hours without your company are sufficient to magnify my loneliness. When I think that barely a week ago we did not even know one another! You cannot begin to imagine the scope of your influence over my humble self.

Please do not think that I get carried away in this manner with every new acquaintance, in the first place because you are much more than an acquaintance, in the second, because I have reached an age and a measure of disenchantment as to give of myself less often and more judiciously than I did when I was a young man.

I want you to know that I find your company endlessly agreeable, and that our meeting could prove to be one of those defining moments which a man encounters only rarely in his lifetime. I do not know what curious reasoning compels me to declare myself thus, since there is nothing that you do not know about me, nor about my feelings for you, since you can read me as one reads a book, because you see right through me, a sensation I find somewhat alarming.

I am certain that I should not reread this letter before sending it, because I would be capable of destroying it at once, overwhelmed by my own foolishness and immodesty. But they say letters written in the heat of the moment are the expression of a profound truth, that one should accept them, as they come but rarely.

This letter is to tell you that I am thinking of you, and that I miss you. Whatever one writes, does one ever come to more than this simple, joyous truth: I think of you, I miss you?

Returning to Illiers is always a strange experience for me. It means coming back, truly, to the childhood that I try to discover in my books, and it is precisely this confrontation between the written and the real that is strange.

In writing about my childhood, I am, for the most part, writing about Illiers. It is here that the story of my father's family begins. It is here that I spent my summer holidays, and, often, my Easter holidays, for almost fifteen years, as a boy and as a young man. Illiers is part of Normandy, and yet somehow part of the Île de France, it is an in-between world of vast monotonous spaces. To get to Illiers, I must take the train to Chartres and change: quite an expedition! Just think: it takes hours to find oneself barely a hundred kilometres from Paris. But I am particularly fond of coming here, of finding the church that towers over the town so commandingly that it has become a character in my book, to find these places where I have walked so often that I carry the memory of them with me everywhere. No doubt, you would not feel about Illiers as I do, because you and I do not share the same childhood; you would perhaps be bored by these long deserted roads ending always in boundless fields of wheat. You have need of hustle and bustle and Illiers offers little of the sort. It is something very different, as I have said: here are the lost years won back with words, the softness of things restored through patience, the warm light of summer falling on my aged face, making the years fall suddenly away; here is my family, all of them dead, and all of them alive once more.

Simply writing to you about Illiers brings tears to my

eyes. A melancholy takes hold of me, but it is a joyful melancholy all the same. I try to recapture the flavour of a faraway time; you know, that subtle flavour which never fades, which accompanies us always, in silence, in secret, and which we find inadvertently as we turn a corner, in the sweep of a glance, in the murmuring of a forest where once we played many years before. It is an exquisite sadness.

I do not know why I feel the need to speak to you of melancholy in this fashion, you who have asked nothing of me, and who, I believe, are so little disposed to melancholy. Doubtless it is simply that I wish that you were with me in these moments . . . Ah, if I could but revisit my history, my geography, with you by my side, I would be the happiest man in the world . . .

Meanwhile, since such an event is unlikely to occur, I wish only to convey to you all my affection and some affectionate kisses. I shall be in Illiers for several days and, if you have no objection, I shall write to you again.

Your friend, Marcel

Dear Marcel,

It is summer in Paris, bombs are falling and I am horribly alone. Your letter bringing me news of your brief absence saddened me, though it brought me solace to know that despite your absence you think of me a little.

I feel sure that I should not admit this to you, for I know all too well your predisposition to blame yourself, nevertheless, I must say that I would have so liked you to be here, near at hand, as these July days turn sour. I think I would have need of you, of our assignations. I know they would have helped to cheer me in these bleak hours, tinged with sorrow for reasons I cannot easily explain to you.

Nonetheless, I would not wish you to feel in any way obliged to me, since the freedom of others in general, and your freedom most particularly, are of greater import to me than my own. And my distress will surely pass, you know, there is no reason that you should worry.

Here life goes on as usual, as you can imagine, from Father's never-ending lectures to Mother's unseemly whining. It is a familiar state of affairs against which I long ago ceased to rebel. All in all, I am a dutiful son waiting patiently for time to pass, though in truth I do not quite know where I should like it to take me.

No, I do not know Illiers, but, from the way in which you describe it, I do not imagine that I could find there what you return to seek. My past is Paris: I know nothing else. If I were called upon to reminisce, there would be little to say. My attachments are not to places, nor to ancestry. In fact, my only important ties are to the present, to people. Your affection for me ties me to the world. It is knowing that I am in someone's thoughts that causes me to be.

None of this is disheartening, quite the reverse. The heart beats on.

With heartfelt affection,
Vincent

My dear Vincent,

I hasten to reply to your letter which arrived here today and which, as you rightly supposed, has pitched me into the utmost torment. It is true that I sensed in you a sort of despair which moved me deeply. The impassiveness which you affect could so easily give way to a great melancholy. And now it has happened, I am not there, I have chosen precisely this moment to leave your side . . .

You were right: I am eaten up with guilt, but you should know that you need only ask and I shall return immediately. I cannot bear to think of you so sad, and so forlorn. You are kind enough to consider me a friend: remember that a friend's duty is to be there when others are not, to offer a shoulder, a glance, some simple companionship in which one might take comfort. Do not hesitate to make use of me, of our friendship.

Furthermore, you should not hesitate, should you feel able, to tell me of the reasons for your sadness. You know that I ask nothing of you, that I will pose you no questions, in the first place because my upbringing taught me to abstain from posing questions which might prove indelicate, in the second, because I know you will answer only if you so decide, and that your decision will come without my asking. Nonetheless, to be of some little succour, I should need to know a little more.

Whatever you decide, I will respect your choice, and I will always walk beside you, even if we must travel in the utmost silence.

I remain your most devoted,

Marcel

My love,

It is my first day here and my first act is to write to you, for my first thought is of you. My first, and every other.

I realise that this letter, too, is a first – my first love-letter. All around I seem to see new beginnings, a startling thought when you have learned, as I have, that barbarism everywhere, in every age, has but one face, and that this battlefield, with some small differences which are no more than technical advancements, is the same as the battlefields in our history books.

Make no mistake, if everything is new again because you turned my life upside down, because you changed all the rules, nothing has changed here in these mud trenches desiccated by the July sun. The dogged silence, the crippling wait, the frightened faces just a little older now are the same. Even the faces of young men I have never met seem familiar, as though I had seen them somewhere before, because, in the end, all soldiers have the same face, the same numb, worried, worn-out expression. The same grimy necks, the collars of their filthy uniforms turned up, the same cheeks stippled with beard, the same lank hair. To find some hint of humanity, some basic difference between us, you must look into our eyes. And that is precisely what I spend my days doing, Vincent: I stare into their eyes, into the light in their eyes. I know blue eyes that remind me of imaginary seas, green which have given me back a taste of autumn mornings, brown eyes where a fleeting tenderness flickers laced with sadness. I look into the eyes of these soldiers and I struggle to believe we are still alive, that we will manage to stay alive. And I cry. But no one laughs at my tears. In war, we do not mock the man who cracks. We stay silent, we look away, we wait for the tears to stop; this is the silent wait for all tears to end.

And then, the moment comes when I close my eyes so that I can remember yours, can call up their brilliance. I know the glimmer in your eyes when we meet, when we kiss, when we sit in silence together, when we wake, and the glimmer is different in each circumstance, but the eyes are the same. I concentrate on those eyes, I try to think of nothing else. I know this thought protects me, helps me to live a little longer, keeps me from harm. That's it: it is as though you are watching me, you seem to say, be calm, nothing will happen to you, nothing; not while I watch over you.

Stupid, isn't it? Grotesquely stupid. But still, that is how it is. That is all I wanted to say. That, and that I love you, although I know you do not want to see me write those words. But what else could I write that would come close to the truth? Yes, Vincent, I love you. That's all.

Arthur

Arthur,

I write this not knowing whether you will receive my letter. I cannot understand how letters can be carried on to a battlefield. Truly, it is an unfathomable mystery to me. But they tell me that the military authorities perform heroic feats so that letters arrive at their destinations, because such letters have a positive effect on troop morale, and of course it is easier for me to believe that they do. It is important to know that my words will not be lost, that you will read them. As I write, I imagine you reading these words.

I am not sure that the military would be happy to learn that they are assuming full responsibility for carrying a dispatch from a young man of sixteen to his lover in the trenches, and I am delighted at the thought that we have hoodwinked them. I have always thought that it is frivolity that saves us.

You might find it shocking to speak of frivolity like this, but I know that you have come to understand me. Provocation could not be further from my thoughts. I say things as they occur to me, without really thinking about them, as a child throws toys for his parents to pick up without meaning any harm. I can be serious, but I would not wish to be grim. I side with life, always.

I remember your eyes, too, with an exactness that is almost troubling. I remember every nuance of your gaze, each minute, barely perceptible shift. And within that 'barely perceptible' are great upheavals, shifts from light to darkness, from joy to sorrow, from poise to diffidence. I know that I have seen in your eyes what others have been unable to see, what others have not thought to look for.

I have my whole day to think of you. I do nothing else. It is my sole occupation. My parents leave me to myself. The city is empty and the last inhabitants of our deserted metropolis seem to be holed up, waiting for the next bombing raid. The sun filters through the shutters of my room where you are no longer and where I can still find your presence in every object. It is idleness, a gentle, melancholy indolence.

All the same, from time to time I write to my friend Marcel, of whom I have not spoken before because we had better things to do than to talk about my friends when we were together. And lest you be needlessly jealous, I should point out that Marcel is a writer, he is old and quite ugly. But he is, too, a considerate and charming man whose company helps me to get through the days. And so, alone in our beloved capital city, I send letters to the provinces hoping to dispel some part of my loneliness. I like to think of the words as they travel to those to whom they are intended. These words journey to tell you of the shiver that runs through me each time I must leave you on your field of desolation. They come to tell you . . .

Vincent

My dear Marcel,

I wanted to keep everything to myself, but I realise now that it is impossible and, naturally, you are someone – perhaps the only one – I can trust.

I wanted to keep everything to myself because it is the nature of love stories to be secret, because it is in secret that they flourish, or so I have been told.

Of course, a secret is a form of etiquette, a sort of shyness. It is a silence which protects us from the scrutiny of others whose judgement we cannot know in advance, which may prove benevolent, dispassionate or malicious.

A secret is also a form of procrastination, a means of waiting to be certain that what one is hiding is truly worth concealing. It is that delicious impatience which precedes confession.

Lastly, a secret may serve to conceal something which cannot be spoken of without creating something of a stir. It is a means of avoiding public outrage when what is concealed seems, for example, contrary to good conduct.

But there can be no secrets between true friends, precisely because one does not wish to hide from true friends; with them one longs to confess this thing which burns inside because we know that they will understand.

I think that I can honestly say that you are such a friend. Therefore I will waste no more time, but tell you that I have met a young man, a schoolmaster by profession, a soldier of twenty-one engaged in the Great War, and that I harbour for this man, and he for me, the deepest and, dare I say, the most passionate feelings.

I must tell you, Marcel, that this is, too, a physical passion.

This is my terrible, my great, my paltry, my marvellous secret. This is what makes me so joyful and so sad. The joy of sudden, straightforward happiness. The sadness of unjust and painful separation. There, Marcel, now you know all. Or, rather, you know the lion's share. What remains, by which I mean the words, the gestures, the looks, you can imagine without the need for me to say more.

I shall understand if you are shocked, for I believe I can understand what is scandalous in the love of a boy for another boy, what is scandalous in a youth of barely sixteen physically offering himself, what is scandalous in a story which implicates one of our soldiers at a time when our armies have enough to concern them without possible scandal. Please believe that it was not my intention to shock, or to create a scandal. I thought of none of these things at the moment when, that first time, I put my arms around him. I did not feel myself constrained – and in this I was perhaps mistaken – by any moral precepts when his lips met mine that very first time. I did not feel that what I was doing was wrong, nor do I feel so now. I am far removed from all feelings of guilt because I am closest to the feeling of love. However, I accept that you may decide that what I have done is wrong, even if I believe that you are likely to acknowledge my right to be different.

I anxiously await your judgement. I hope for your compassion, and perhaps your support. I am, come what may, your affectionate friend.

Vincent de l'Étoile

My dear child,

I must begin by confessing that, far more than I suspected at our first meeting, you are a source of constant wonderment to me. I sensed that you were not one of those dreary, conceited adolescents who are the stuff of which tedious husbands are made, nor one of those flamboyant dandies destined to become repulsive reactionaries. I suspected that behind your mask of superb indifference a fire burned; that in spite of your manner which seemed unmoved by anything, you could be inflamed by passion. But from that to what was revealed in your letter, which arrived in Illiers today, required a leap of imagination which I would never have thought to make.

Unquestionably, you are one of a kind, and you should know that I say this with regret as one who would have wished to see in himself some likeness.

Of course, simple morality obliges me to condemn most severely the dishonourable indiscretions which you describe. Think: a young man of good family succumbing to the abominable vice of the Greeks. In itself, this is enough to have you banished for ever. But what is worse, and you were right to emphasise it: this deplorable inversion has manifested itself while you are but a child, and you feel compelled to consummate it with one of our valiant soldiers now at war, whose conduct should in all things be exemplary. No, clearly there is nothing in this tale that does not arouse indignation and even revulsion. I should say, as one so often reads in the columns in our newspapers: let us have no more of this, Sir, I want nothing more to do with you. But, obviously, if you have chosen to confide in me it is because you are confident of my reaction and of my judgement, because you presume I am not likely to dispense some summary and expedient justice. And, of course, you are right.

I do not have the preconceptions of the bigot, and I have more faith in mankind than I do in a morality in which everything is proscribed. I believe that one is right to pursue happiness, and I am quick to applaud those who believe that they have found it, even when they have found it by a roundabout route.

Do not believe, however, that I absolve you, Vincent. Absolution is neither my prerogative, nor my custom. I leave you to your conscience; alone, free – completely free – marvellously, dangerously free to choose, or at the very least, to follow your inclinations.

But I believe that I must warn against passions of this kind, which one feels so keenly at this most ardent age, when body and mind are changing and one feels disposed to new experiences. I have known such passions, I know how enchanting and exciting they are, but I know, too, how painful they can be. I know that one must suffer the censure of others, their contempt, their spite or, simply, their science against our supposed ignorance, their moral strength against our supposed misdeeds, their righteousness faced with our depravity, their virtue faced with our perversion. I know that one must come to terms with the rejection of those to whom one feels most drawn, to whom we offer an affection which goes unrequited. I know the solitude and the suffering. I know the imprisonment. I would not wish such things for you because, as I have told you, you are dear to my heart.

Do not expose yourself needlessly to censure; do not recklessly leave yourself vulnerable to the cruelty of offers. Be wary of offers, often honestly and sincerely made, which will lay you open to the most terrible suffering.

By the same token, I am admiring and jealous of your magnificent independence, of your ability to defy what is forbidden without hesitating as to right and wrong, of your freedom in the world of the flesh, of your talent for courting the greatest dangers and the most exalted pleasure. I salute your courage, although you do not feel that what you have done is courageous.

And I wish to tell you that, more even than yesterday, I am, of course, your friend, I am by your side, I will be with you in the happy moments as in the melancholy hours. I remain he who is writing a book for you.

Your Marcel

Marcel,

I want to thank you from the bottom of my heart for your letter which may well have saved my life. My secret had become so oppressive that it was absolutely vital that I confess it. Thank you for making it possible for me to do so.

I could not have imagined how much I would change. I believed that people do not change, truly change. I believed that my nonchalance would always be part of me, it is so much my hallmark, this indifference which in truth simply allows me to eschew unnecessary constraints. The simple idea that nothing is important and everything is possible.

I believed in this wholeheartedly, in that way that only children can believe. Is this what it means to become an adult? Giving up the beliefs which reassure us, which help us to survive?

I was mistaken. I have noted how much these two adventures I am living, these two encounters which occurred at almost the same moment, have transformed my state of mind, making me at once exhilarated and troubled, emotions utterly alien to me.

You are, of course, quite right to be wary of the kind of passion I have come to know all too well, and to warn me that the future may bring disappointment. But how can one live other than in the present? And why should one sacrifice present happiness for a sorrow that tomorrow may bring?

You are right, Marcel, and yet I shall not heed your advice. I want to live. I want to feel the pulse of life. That excitement that brings both pleasure and terror. I want to feel joy, even at the risk of sadness.

And is not my suffering itself astounding? The pain of being separated from him. He was hardly mine when he was taken from me again. And no one can tell me when he will be given back to me. You know, it takes great love to weather such pain. Great love. If I try to control my emotions, the pain will overwhelm me, it will sweep me aside. You must understand that I do not wish to control anything, on the contrary, I wish to give myself up to this flux.

I will need you, Marcel, in this maelstrom. I will need your friendship, your understanding, your support. I will need you to guide me. I believe I can understand the affection you bear for men. I will need you to tell me how one lives one's life with this love of men. Because I may as well confess, I believe that my love for Arthur comes from deep inside me; it is not an infatuation, nor is it experimentation, but a definite preference.

Will you accept this role as guide, as a fair and impartial friend? Will you talk to me as a man who knows does to a young man who does not know?

With great affection

Vincent

My love,

Here there is only the uninterrupted thunder of shellfire. The yellow earth is battered, pot-holed and cracked, and columns of smoke rise from the nearby hills. Small fires start everywhere and the ground trembles. Everything is topsy-turvy. It is a bedlam beyond words. From time to time, when the barrage stops, we can make out the bodies of our men lying only metres away. Some blown to pieces, unrecognisable, covered in blood and dirt, others seem miraculously intact and it takes a moment to make out the thin trickle of blood running from the temple or the chest, the tell-tale sign that there is no life in this young body, still warm, aching to be held. The lulls in the fighting are always short. The shelling never stops for long. And with the shelling, the offensives begin again, each one more desperate, more murderous than the last. It is a grisly carnage. This massacre is a grotesque, consummately absurd game. But sometimes I wonder if the absurdity, the cacophony, simply make it easier for us to go over the top, again and again, into battle, because they defy all reason, because they make it easier not to think. Here, if you think, you end up turning your gun on yourself. Everything is so wretched, so grim. No one can imagine what it's like. The ones who tell our story when this is over won't be able to find words, because there are no words for this. What little they can describe, that they can recount, will seem unbelievable or meaningless.

They will be alone, utterly alone with their indelible, unspeakable memories of this ordeal.

I know I shouldn't talk to you about this, that it only serves to worry you, but how can I not bear witness? How could anyone keep all this inside? It's impossible, can you understand that? Impossible to say nothing. Impossible to pass over in silence this loathsome spectacle in which we are the unwilling players. Impossible not to try and give an account of the daily horror. We are steeped in it so completely that it becomes a part of us, until finally it is unshakeable. It surrounds us, like a dead man's greatcoat we are forced to wear. It is something which is over us, beside us, against us, and yet, at the same time, it is us. Something prowling about us.

I could not write to you without speaking of this, unless I were to lie, to hide the truth from you, to hide our truth, and I do not want a lie, however small, nor the least flaw, to come between us. Even in the midst of the rank stain that is this war, one pure thing will survive – the love between us. That one pure thing helps me to survive. And it flares up and breaks free in me every night.

I'd like to believe this purity will help us overcome the enemy we have been sent to face, but simple honesty forces me to recognise that: omnipotent though purity may be, it cannot help us here, in the barbarity in which we are engaged. It is a suit of armour made of paper, an imaginary shield. Our love is silk, it won't stop bullets here. We must be careful it does not become my shroud.

Excuse me, please excuse me for sending you this hopelessness, this sadness which is the only thing I have to give. Remember that, even if my spirit is troubled and my body threatened, my feelings have not changed from that first time I held you, from that last time I held you. Remember that alongside this sadness is an equal happiness in knowing that I have you in my heart. Remember that one can be the happiest of men, the saddest of men in the same thought.

Lastly, I wanted to tell you that I am happy that you can speak to the friend you mentioned in your letter. That you are not so alone. It is important to have friends. They are the meaning we give to life. Write to me again of him. In knowing him a little better, I feel I come a little closer to you.

I will write again as soon as I can. Take care. I love you.

Arthur

Arthur,

Here is something I still think of as a miracle: your letters reach me. As I write these words, I realise that the only things which reach me are your letters. Nothing else touches me.

Your letters are like a wound and a caress. I understand all the more the ever-present danger which hangs over you, and more, too, how much I miss you.

If you only knew how much I miss you. Every moment I miss you. Every move I make is incomplete. Every word I speak is met with silence. Every place I walk I feel an empty space. Every look is blinded. Every minute a throb of regret.

Everywhere, I can smell your smell, your wildness.

Sometimes I believe I weep. There are tears. I cannot hold them back. They well up before I can stop them. In these moments I feel desolate. In these moments, the memories are unbearable, I need to obliterate memory, to forget everything and return to that pure state before this began.

And then, just as suddenly, I remember that this is the most wonderful thing that has ever happened to me. I need to remember everything, learn by heart each tiny detail. I write everything in exercise books so as not to forget any detail.

Besides, I have the watch you left behind. It is the one thing that I have, the one thing which connects me to you. It is the bond, the only physical bond I have with you. It is an ironic stroke of luck, in that it is this which allows me precisely to measure what keeps you from me. With this watch, I am aware of time passing between us, while knowing nothing of the time that remains before we are, I hope, together again.

How is it possible to have been with you, to be without you? How can I have lost you? From time to time, I think, against all reason: I should have kept him here, prevented him from leaving, run away with him, made a deserter of him. After all, what do I care about the fate of the country? What matters to me is us. Us before them, before all of them. The thought never lasts long because I quickly realise how absurd, how childish it is. But it lasts just long enough to be painful, to leave a deep wound from which it takes me hours to recover.

It is only because I believe we will not be apart for ever that I am alive at all.

Sometimes, that single thought helps me to be less frightened.

To curb my fear, there is also the other, he who is here, close at hand, to whom I can talk, he who reassures me, who helps me bear your absence. There is Marcel.

Marcel, as I told you, is a writer. A famous writer. Maybe you know his name. To me, however, he is an affable individual in whom I believe I can confide my heartache as well as the profound happiness that you have brought into my life.

I have decided, in the end, to read his books to get to

know him better. He writes wonderfully about childhood. Words that are tender and melancholy which paint a picture of a world I should like to have known. I should like his past to have been my own, as I think he would like my future to be his.

I am beginning to realise how much Marcel is, above all, a man turned entirely towards the past, as though he were looking for some golden age that is lost for ever, as though he were trying to unearth fugitive emotions which he longs to feel once more. His work surveys the past, and he himself seems quite unfamiliar with the revolutions which have taken place these last years, especially in the field of art. He is an *aficionado* of Vermeer and Chardin, but has nothing whatever to say about Rimbaud or Picasso. Marcel is the antithesis of a 'modern'. In spite of this, one would not think to reproach him for this because one intuits, apart from his nostalgia, his keen sensitivity to suffering, his conviction that his happiest years are behind him and that those years left to him serve only to bear witness to that lost time.

I feel a great tenderness towards him, perhaps because of the sadness he affects, but also because of his unqualified respect for the freedom of others, his manner of allowing others to become what they are. He is a great comfort to me.

As I finish this letter, which will be quickly followed by another since it is in writing these letters that I feel closest to you, I want you to remember that Marcel is taking care of me, and that his presence helps me to endure your absence.

With all my love

Vincent

My dear child,

My thoughts turn again to you, still vexed that I have not been able to be by your side in these (perhaps) decisive moments of your life, beleaguered as I am by a plethora of administrative difficulties here in Illiers.

You do me the honour of considering that my advice may be of value to you and for this I thank you. I hasten to tell you that I am not altogether certain that parts of my counsel will not necessarily prove injudicious, since my experience does not entirely correspond with your queries. Furthermore, I know that it is best to refrain from offering advice, for when such advice is misguided, one is toying with the lives of others, a game in which I want no part.

However, since you have solicited my advice, I offer these few thoughts which I believe to be true and which, I hope, may prove useful in your deliberations as to the path your future life will take.

Firstly, remember that inversion – since it is thus we must name what you have come to know – inversion is still considered a crime. I am sure that I need not remind you of the momentous trials chronicled in these last years which prove, if proof were needed, that the paragons of bourgeois, Judaeo-Christian virtue occupy the moral high ground and it is they who decide for us what is good and what is evil. Take heed, dear Vincent, barbarism and folly are not the sole preserve of the battlefield, they are just as apparent in our books of law and in the minds of those who govern us. I beg you, in each of your actions, to bear in mind this loathsome truth. I know that you have no fear of bringing scandal upon yourself nor upon your family, nonetheless, I would find it somewhat disagreeable to be obliged to visit you in gaol. For that is precisely what you risk, you know: gaol. One does not play the fool with such things. These days, it were better to beat an old woman to death in France than to fall in love with a boy when you your-self are a boy.

There is something which I wish to say to you besides, and which I do not doubt you will not wish to hear, far less to believe: I have come to the conviction that those who love and those who are happy are not the same.

I believe in fact – forgive me – that love is unavoidably the root of unhappiness.

You must learn that the one you love is, above all, he who causes or will cause you pain, because sooner or later he will dissemble, openly or obliquely, consciously or unconsciously, in whole or in part. Yes, inevitably he will dissemble and you will find yourself powerless to possess him completely. Possession: an ugly word, is it not? I can hear you from here. Nonetheless, in the end, love is a matter of possession, whether one likes it or not. Do you love me? Do you love someone other than me?

Worse still: it is precisely because the other holds

back that one loves him all the more. It is struggle which feeds passion and gives it form. It is trouble. It is the eternal need to seduce, to convince, to bind, to hold on which is the food of love. And so, we find ourselves in a vicious circle, ever failing just when we believe we have triumphed, routed in the end because it was impossible that we should win. Love engenders its own destruction.

I would also like to say that, when I assert that those who love and those who are happy are not the same, I am simply calling attention to the fact that, often, in love, there is one who gives and one who takes, one who offers himself and one who chooses, one who reveals and one who conceals, one who suffers and one who survives. It is a cruel game because the dice are loaded. It is a dangerous game because inexorably one must lose.

I expect that you will resent me just a little for inflicting these supposed truths upon you, truths which at worst you believe to be foolishness, at best, to be realities which do not apply to you. Of course you will not believe that what I have said applies to you, you may even be tempted to accuse me of being a killjoy. For my part, I would not blame you for your mistrust nor your rebuke.

Vincent, you are sixteen and I am forty-five. Of the two, I am the one who knows. Of the two, you are the one who is right. When one is sixteen, one is always right. What matter if what one believes at sixteen is true or not. What one believes when one is sixteen is more powerful than any truth.

Nevertheless, I owe it to my sense of honesty to say to you what I have said. I have long passed the age of telling people what they wish to hear. Such things are appropriate only to salon chatter, and I would like to think that our discussions are worth more than the idle conversation of the salon.

And I owe it to our friendship to tell you that, for myself, I have been devastated by the loss of someone close to me. Devastated to the point where *each time I boarded a taxi, I wished with all my heart that the omnibus coming towards me would fell me.* Devastated to the point where I wished to die to end the terrible, unspeakable, insuperable suffering which I felt because of the loss of someone dear to me. This admission should tell you how much I loved him. *And it is not enough to say that I loved him, I adored him.* And yet, I could not say with certainty that the affection he felt for me was truly sincere, for it was fused with a significant degree of self-interest, and, on many occasions I was made to suffer gruelling pangs of jealousy through his thoughtlessness, his fickleness, sometimes his cruelty. A pathetic story, don't you think? It is the story of my life.

I hope that you may prove me wrong, that you will love your Arthur and be loved by him and that nothing will come to thwart that love. Quite simply, I wish you to be happy, for you deserve as much.

Write to me, dear child. Speak of me to him, and speak to me of you.

With great affection,

Your Marcel

Arthur,

I am writing again, though I have not received a letter from you, I hover between the fear of imagining that if I have received nothing it is because you have sent nothing (and why should you send nothing?) and (unwarranted) anger at the tardiness with which letters are delivered in wartime.

I am writing because it is impossible not to write, impossible to remain silent, impossible not to try and reach you with words, impossible to banish you from my thoughts, and when my thoughts tend towards obsession then writing becomes a release, a therapy.

I am writing because the time it takes for your letters to reach me is longer than I can bear before you return to me, and so they are a measure of my impatience, they chart the inexorable rise of my anxiety. I write, because in writing I am with you. It is an attempt to be close to you. It fails inasmuch as a letter cannot lessen the distance between us, but succeeds in that at the moment of writing I think only of you, of nothing else but that which you are, I am focused absolutely on you.

To get to know you, I talked to your mother. I succeeded in approaching, in speaking to this woman whom I have never done other than greet in the morning when she arrives and again when she leaves. I did this thing that I had never done before: I spoke to her. It took a lot of nerve and I had to make several attempts before words came at last from my mouth. I had to wait until we were alone and until she was not busy on some errand for my mother. I had to overcome my shame that in all these years I had never spoken to her, and that I was doing so now only because I felt a terrible need. I had to overcome, also, the possibility that you might chide me for this, the possibility that you might disapprove. The task was exhausting, and several times I almost abandoned it.

And then, this morning, without my truly having planned it, overjoyed at the happy coincidence of her availability and my idling in the drawing room, free of my parents who had gone to see my grandmother in Auteuil, I finally decided to approach your mother. At the moment I uttered the first word I was breathless, like someone on the edge of an abyss. So my first sentence was all but inaudible. Your mother must have thought me a very stupid young man, though, naturally, she did not let her feelings show. At first, we talked about nothing much, so much so that I can barely remember the platitudes we exchanged. It was probably something about the weather and this endless summer.

Then, I said: have you had any news from your son? At that moment, she tensed and the look on her face was both serious and tender, and she began by saying: a letter arrived yesterday. He says he is well. And then, she seemed to want to add something, but in the end, she said nothing. For my part, I did not want the conversation to end and yet I did not know what to say to her.

There we were, in a waltz of hesitation.

We were silent, but it was not uncomfortable. It was not an embarrassed silence. More a reverential silence, but also an expression of great propriety. We were not separated by this silence for we both knew that there was something more to say, something else to share. When I looked up, I saw that she was looking at me, not questioningly but thoughtfully, rather. And in her eyes, then, I saw that she knew everything without anything needing to be said; that she had worked everything out, that she understood this story, our story. It was almost imperceptible, the attentiveness of her gaze, the glow in her face, a motherly expression that I have never seen in my own mother, and a sort of distress, too, or rather a distress call. Here. Here in the middle of the drawing room we stood, she and I, saying nothing to one another and it was more than words could say.

When she left the room, she turned one last time and said simply: the next time you hear from him, would you be so kind as to let me know? I nodded slightly in acquiescence. When she had gone, I began to cry. Inexplicably, I wept.

I believed that I had just witnessed one of the most dignified and poignant moments of my life.

Tell me you don't hate me, Arthur. Tell me that you don't think that what I did was wrong. I need your forgiveness. I am so alone here, so confused. I have to cope with my loneliness, with my confusion. And I don't know what is right and what is wrong. Tell me that you don't blame me.

Even Marcel, gentle, kind-hearted Marcel has warned me so sternly against passions of this kind that by the time I finish his letters I feel troubled. If you should reproach me too, I shall not know what to do any more.

I shall wait to hear from you like a sailor's wife waiting on the quay. I love you.

Vincent

My Vincent,

Before I do anything, before I reply to your letter, before I tell you again how much I love you, I want to tell you about Alexis Guérande.

I must tell you about Alexis Guérande.

Alexis would have been twenty in a few days – on August 17th, to be precise. He was born in Quimper, the only son of a washerwoman and a baker from Finistère. Something of a poet, Alexis was a solitary, somewhat taciturn young man, who missed the countryside and his parents terribly and felt a longing for the ocean and for his family. He talked little, and kept himself out of sight, away from the others as though he were afraid, as though their company was a danger to him, which is probably why I was drawn to him more than to any of the others.

As I told you before, war contrives impulsive friendships and snatches them away just as quickly as it creates them. We are never truly intimate with anyone, yet at times we feel a certain affection for some, an affection which would probably not run so deep were we civilians. This contradiction is all the more evident since, while we feel a desperate need to be close to someone, we are wary of getting too close, because we cannot forget that from one minute to the next it could end brutally in a rain of shells which we had not seen coming.

This is the kind of affection I had for Alexis, honest but without illusions; intense, but aware of its precarious nature; something strong but fragile. And I am weak enough to think that my affection was reciprocated, that Alexis enjoyed my company, and found in me someone he could talk to, perhaps even confide in. We talked a lot, he and I, in the long sickening hours of waiting between two skirmishes, two bursts of shelling.

When I think of him, I immediately hear his voice, quiet and unhurried, each word measured, each confession both a gift of himself and a manner of forgetting himself. I can hear him talking to me about Brittany, of his childhood haunts, of the humid weather, the morning mists, the simplicity of a life lived with mother and father, of his happiness I suppose. I can hear his voice whispering in the trenches.

We were sent together to the front. In the midst of the terrifying din, in the indescribable panic, we fought side by side, advancing the front line. Because you know we have to advance at all costs, win back inches of ground from the enemy, reach the barbed wire a hundred metres ahead. We must move forward, crouch, resting one knee on the ground, stop, aim, perhaps kill someone, set off again, hope that we are not in someone else's sights. And every time we advance, we lose dozens of men. The bullets whistle past and find their mark in dozens of hearts. The incessant thunder of cannonfire flings bodies into the air, hurls bodies that are crippled, mangled, mutilated into the tracery of the shellfire. To escape the slaughter, we drag ourselves into holes and try to huddle into the dirt waiting for the moment when the firing stops. And when at last everything is calm – if one can call that petrifying silence calm – when it is calm once more we hear the feeble voices of the wounded calling for their mothers like some memory of childhood, the voices of the dying begging to be saved or begging to be killed, we can hear prayers, from who knows where in the wreckage, incantations which drift off with the smoke of exploded shells. And then the pestilential stench reaches us from the field strewn with corpses, the stink of a slaughterhouse mingled with gunpowder. Make no mistake, death has a smell. And if I should survive, I will certainly recognise it if ever I smell it again. Then, when we haul ourselves out of our makeshift shelters we see the corpses everywhere, these bodies in curious poses, sometimes entwined as in some love scene which seems incongruous here, the frozen image of war.

That is what I lived through with Alexis Guérande, a twenty-year-old soldier. That and the nights burning like a furnace, the shame and the cowardice of retreat when the enemy was stronger, and other things too which it is useless to relate, for one tires of everything, even of recounting atrocities which have with time become horribly ordinary.

Alexis Guérande is dead. Alexis Guérande died this morning by my side. He died from a stray bullet to the head during a lull when the fighting had stopped and our guard was down. A single bullet, lodged in his left temple, nothing more, something clear-cut, like a glimmer of pure diamond which left a sudden red puncture at the tip of his eyebrow. He died instantly. Alexis didn't notice a thing, didn't see it coming. Just after, a fine trickle of blood ran down from his mouth. His eyes stayed open. His pale blue eyes, his beautiful eyes suddenly empty, frozen. It only took a second: the bullet's impact, the trickle of blood, the eyes frozen.

On a battlefield, you grow accustomed to death, you recognise it easily. You immediately understand what has happened. You recognise it as a misfortune, an injustice fated to happen. You say nothing. It hurts a little and then you move on, you keep going. If you have no stomach for death, if you cannot carry on as before, you will die. I've seen dozens of soldiers die. I keep on going.

And yet this morning, when I realised Alexis was dead, for the first time I thought that I couldn't go on, that this was one death too many, that I could not get through this ordeal, that it was beyond me. As I ran my hand over his face to close his eyes, I thought that I wasn't able to carry on any more. Alexis's skin had the softness of a young man of twenty. That soft skin, that smooth face under my fingers made me want to weep, to give up. I supposed the death of Alexis Guérande was reason enough to give up. I thought that the death of a young man of twenty, with such soft skin, was reason enough to stop trying to survive, to stop trying to make it out alive. I thought the world made no sense if young men of twenty with such soft skin could die.

That is what happened just now.

Just that.

Just a death.

A world destroyed.

Now you can understand a little better the state of mind of the person writing to you.

And, thinking of the parents Alexis left behind, thinking about their all-consuming grief, of their heart-breaking mourning, of their shattered lives, I thought that this was something which I would not wish to leave to you. What use is a promise which offers only suffering, only a helpless waiting for an uncertain death, only a kind of widowhood without a marriage. It is wrong to offer so little hope.

I don't know exactly what your friend Marcel said, but I agree with him when he 'warned you against passions of this kind'. I think I understand his intentions when he tries to spare you any possible disappointment and suffering. I think you should listen to him.

What's more, what you told me about my mother didn't make me angry, in fact, I think she feels less alone now that she has 'conversed' with you, but it reinforced my wish to spare those who are waiting for me any news which might cause them irreparable pain, or such grief as might take years to overcome.

I cannot ask that of the people I love, of those whom I care about most. Your pain is ten times greater than mine, believe me. So this unreal story in which, against our will, we play out our allotted roles, makes everyone unhappy.

I want to say that it is perhaps best if you forget me, that it is better for you to turn towards the future, because you have your whole life ahead of you; that you find new loves who will not make you suffer needlessly. To write these words to you takes extraordinary courage and reveals a despair beyond all measure, but it means that reason must triumph, that reason can triumph still before we are all utterly mad.

To love someone is, above all, to protect him from blows that might mortally wound him.

To be loved is to be able to expect the loved one to save himself before it is too late, to cut off his infected arm so that the gangrene does not spread and kill him.

Don't write. If you don't write, I will know that you have accepted the merits of my reasoning.

I will love you to my last breath.

Arthur

My Arthur,

I am writing. Your letter has just arrived and, without a moment's thought, I am writing. I cannot bear for you to think for another moment that I could accept your reasoning.

What you have asked of me is unacceptable and, quite simply, impossible.

One cannot just decide to forget the man one loves. One has no means to do so. Even if one wished to – and I fervently do not wish to – one simply could not do so.

We are together. Do you understand that? We are one. I do not want to find new loves. And I am ready to take any blows. I am writing this in a muddle, I'm sorry, but I have to tell you that you are wrong, that life is stronger, that the bonds between us are stronger, that war is nothing, that you will come back, that you will survive, that we will survive.

I would endure any suffering, I would take on all of them if need be, because I am blessed with every happiness.

And I want you to remember every minute, every second, that I am here, that I am here for you alone, so that you can hold fast for a second, a minute longer, each minute until the end of the war. So that, in the end, you will have to come back to me.

A dead soldier truly is a world destroyed. But two

bodies tumbling between warm sheets are a world reborn. Think about rebirth, about regeneration.

Don't die. Don't die.

Vincent

(letter arrived at its destination, 4 September, 1916)

My dear boy,

In a few days I shall finally be able to quit Illiers for Paris and so I shall have the joy of seeing you again, of listening to you tell me of your life and, perhaps, your loves.

Do you not feel that there is something heart-rending about these dying days of August, whose scurrying storm-clouds seem to herald a menacing autumn? Sometimes I feel as though we shall never come through this war, and the foul weather we have had these last days seems to call it to mind. I know I should not say such things to you who are impatient for this war to end, since it will mark the return of your lover, it is simply my way of cautioning you against false hopes, of hopes that run contrary to good sense, and I believe it my responsibility, since it is a well-known fact that I have responsibilities to you, to prepare you for the worst so that you may be agreeably surprised when the best comes to pass.

No doubt you will resent me for these ill omens or for my words of warning. After all, who am I to permit myself such liberties with you? To this I would respond once more that I am one who has suffered death. I am one who knows loneliness, absence and vain hope better than most. I would not wish such torments on you. You are at an age where such suffering is particularly to be avoided. It is, one might say, an obligation on your part.

Trust the cynical old man that I have become and who loves you as a father, a brother, a friend.

I kiss you, Vincent, I embrace you in the hope that the force of my embrace will give you the courage you need.

I will see you very shortly.

Marcel

From the Major of the 10th company, 77th infantry regiment

Madame Blanche Valès
32 rue des Plantes
Paris XIVe arrondissement

Verdun, 3 September 1916

Madame,

It is with great regret that I must inform you of the death of your son, Arthur Valès, second-class soldier in my company. The aforementioned met his death during valiant combat to regain territory seized by the enemy.

You should know that our soldiers are engaged in a heroic struggle, here and throughout the country, to restore to France her integrity and her honour.

I would like to tell you that this country owes and will forever owe him a debt of gratitude.

His remains will be conveyed by the military authorities as soon as practicable to such place as is nominated by you.

Please accept, Madame, my most sincere condolences, both in a personal capacity and on behalf of the French Army.

Major George Gallois

Marcel
He is dead.
He is dead and already my life is over.
Vincent

BOOK THREE

LOSS

The mother is here. She stands before me, taut with grief. Her tautness resembles the stiffness of a corpse. It is not an expression of dignity, though I do not doubt for a moment that this is a woman of consummate dignity. It is the stillness of absolute suffering, the bearing of one struggling with death, struggling not to throw herself from a window, here, now, without truly knowing why she does not throw herself from a window. It is the bearing of one who has lost everything, who has nothing before her but death. Because, in truth, there is nothing now to wait for but death. That is the one thing which will happen. That will be the final experience. And even that will not be an experience. Rather, a formality, a fact, a relief, a logical conclusion. The mother knows that her own death will pass unnoticed.

The mother is here. She is drained of colour as though her face was fashioned from wax, as though all light has been extinguished, as though shadows have crumpled her face, as though the darkness has taken her. It is clear that her pale skin will never be white again, that hereafter the orphaned mother will always have this face, that it will never change, that this greyness is fixed, like some ferrous matter, frozen for all eternity. If she lives a few years more her face will become more wrinkled, more furrowed, but it will not be a transformation, but a slow evolution, a waning, a methodical encroachment of shadows.

The mother is here. She is silent. More than that: she

is silence. She is abstraction. No word escapes her, no sound. She is incapable of uttering a sound, as if she were forbidden. Besides, she does not try to speak, she accepts this muteness which has been thrust upon her, she welcomes it like a blessing. What could she say? And she knows that faced with her silence no one will dare to speak. No one will dare address her. Besides, what could anyone say?

The mother is here. Her presence is all but unbearable. We cannot help but wish that this woman shrouded in suffering, enclosed in suffering, were not here. We would rather not confront this presence with which we can find no common ground. We are crushed by her presence, diminished by it. And yet there is no rebuke in her presence, just the terrible weight of a life shattered, in ruins.

The mother is here. We turn our eyes from her. We do this thing immediately, we turn away. We do not even wish to see her. We do not wish to risk meeting her eyes, to find ourselves face to face with her. We feel an absurd, inexplicable guilt, and also the clear, unsettling impression that here is reason enough for madness, reason enough to hurl oneself from a window. There are tears. The moment one looks at her, there are tears. We are overwhelmed by her suffering.

It continues for a long time. The mother, here. It lasts an eternity, an infinity, a handful of minutes. Each second peels away, quantifiable, detaches itself distinctly from that which preceded it. The time that passes becomes a burden. It continues for a long time. The mother, here.

I must leave, flee this room where she stands. I must draw back from this woman who gave birth to Arthur. It is too much for me. Her presence brings me back to the original purity of my grief, to the limitless depths of my sadness.

But, then, suddenly, it is she who holds me back. It is she who suddenly breaks her silence. She says: stay, I beg you. Precisely this. These are the words she speaks: stay, I beg you. Her voice is a mournful, ghostly drawl. No doubt she cannot help but speak in this voice. She cannot help but speak in a voice which tries to hold her sobs in check. She must modulate her voice to avoid weeping, or at least to rein in her emotion. And suddenly, her voice is commanding, the voice of one whose orders one would not think to challenge. Her voice demands respect, though in the normal hierarchy, as governess of this house, she should be respectful, submissive. This voice strikes me, I can almost hear Arthur's tone in it. A voice from beyond the grave.

Suddenly I stop. I abandon any thoughts of flight. I realise that to run would be futile, that the time has come to face what I have tried, unconsciously, to hide even from myself. I turn towards her. She says nothing, she does not think to apologise for the brusqueness of her manner or the unusual nature of her request. This is no longer the kind of relationship she has with me. This is what she is saying in refusing to apologise, that our relationship is no longer that of master and servant. In this I realise she is correct.

She says: I will talk to you. Afterwards I will not talk of this again. Not a word.

Can you understand how much I need to talk, to say everything, to say it aloud just once then never speak again? It is an obligation, a duty. Afterwards, it will be over.

Can you understand – I have to do this? I can't keep it all inside, though I've been doing that for years. It may seem a paltry secret, but to me it has seemed immense. The enormity of it has kept me silent. But today, I need to scream out this secret.

Can you understand how much I regret saying nothing to my son, though he begged me? Just once I have to talk about this thing I have buried for years or regret will drive me mad.

Can you understand, you are the only person I can talk to now? You are my last link with my son, you are the only witness to this story. It is not simply that you alone can understand, you are at the heart of the story.

Can you understand, I am asking you to take away some small part of my guilt, to tell me that my suffering makes what I did less terrible?

I do not answer. Her questions require no response.

She says: you are sixteen, you should not understand

any of this, but yet I know that you understand everything.

You are the last person I should love, the last person I should think to confide in, but yet, things haven't turned out that way.

Arthur wasn't even fifteen when I realised that he was lost to the love of women, and rather than being shocked, I accepted this knowledge, I resigned myself to it as something which I knew it would be futile to fight. I didn't consider it. But you should not think I was compassionate, or understanding. It was a fact, nothing more. We never spoke of it. Each of us knew that the other knew. It was never a problem, but it was never discussed either. It was simply a knowledge we shared, undisturbed, silent.

I think I knew that he had fallen in love with you before he knew himself. A mother knows such things. She knows how to interpret a son's looks, his manner, the changes in those looks, that manner. Arthur wasn't the same after he had met you. And he talked of you more than he did of anyone. In his letters, he asked for news of you. Some things never lie. A mother notices these things, though they be imperceptible. I knew my son better than I know myself. And you, you noticed nothing.

I listen to the mother speak. Her words absorb me completely. I hear the imperfect used for the first time, and hearing Arthur spoken of in the past tense upsets me more than I can say. I listen to her tell the story, though I have asked nothing. I listen as the story unfurls, ignorant of all that came before me. I hear the mother confess her son's love and I almost faint. I hear that phrase: I knew my son better than I know myself, and I understand what it is to dedicate one's life to another. I say nothing.

She says: I watched you often, though you would never have realised you were being watched. For a long time, I felt you were very young, too young. That's what worried me, much more, say, than the difference in class. I quickly realised that my son would need to live out his love for you, that he wouldn't give it up. I thought: later, perhaps. It happened sooner than I had hoped. He didn't wait. Maybe he couldn't wait.

There was your openness, your honesty, your beauty, the grace with which you carried your sixteen years. I never doubted he had chosen well. You shouldn't think that as his mother I was indulgent. I simply wanted my child to be happy.

The last time he came home, he didn't need to say anything. From the instant I saw him I knew he had made up his mind, that he was going to tell you every-thing, that nothing I could say would stop him. He was seriously determined. He knew what he was doing, what he wanted. He was happy.

And that first night, when he didn't come home, I knew what had happened. I know I shouldn't tell you this, but I wept. I wept because all of a sudden, it had happened, it was true. This difference that set him apart had expressed itself, and for the first time, I couldn't ignore it. It crept up on me. I thought I had grown accustomed to it. But for a mother, the thought of her son's body joined with another boy's is unimaginable. That is precisely what it is: unimaginable.

I think about the courage it takes to speak of a dead son, about the force of will needed simply to voice his name, and then the almost inhuman strength needed to speak, without a hint of censure, of a love one would not have chosen for one's son. I realise that my mother would not be capable of doing what this woman is doing before my eyes, that perhaps no woman would be capable of it. No mother, at least. And I am not at all sure whether in her it inspires admiration or unease.

She says: the rest of the time he was here, he was silent. What I mean is, he did not say anything about what had happened between you. But I realised he was happy. And that happiness, after the butchery he had survived, before the butchery that would surely follow, that happiness was something of which we could not speak.

She says: there is something I want to ask you, that I promised myself I would ask. It is something very personal; I know it is indiscreet, but I think I need to be sure, to know exactly. Did you love him as much as he loved you? Did you realise just how much he loved you and did you feel as he did? I would not wish to think that this has been nothing more for you than an adventure, but I concede that a boy of sixteen, with his whole life ahead of him, thinks of things very differently from a man of twenty-one who is about to die.

For the first time, I will have to speak. For the first time, I will have to tell this story. I am trembling. That is the first thing I feel: my whole body shaking. It is some time before I can say a word; the mother gives me time, her waiting, too, is a sign of understanding. At length, I say: I wasn't prepared for what happened. I expected nothing, I desired nothing, I provoked nothing. One day, it was simply given to me. And all I can say is that I grasped it, without thinking, without a moment's hesitation, it seemed so obvious. Afterwards, I didn't think about it, I didn't think I needed to think about it. I made the most of the time we had, of the intensity of the moment. I was completely honest without ever trying. When he left, I was able to put a name to this. It is the word you yourself used.

The mother seems consoled by this confession. It is a terrible consolation. Love, then, rather than nothing. A boy who loves him rather than a woman he pretended to love. It is not even a consolation, for she is inconsolable. It is simply one less heartache, and in the horror that her life has become, that counts for something.

I wonder if she imagines her son in my arms. However misplaced or unwholesome the thought, it is what

I am thinking. This is the question that springs to mind. I suppose I would like her to have the memories I have, to have the same images of him because these images seem pure to me. And, of course, they are pure. Obviously, she cannot really imagine it, and she probably would not wish to. Then again, she knows the softness of his skin as I do, the force of his embrace. I know that we share a body.

Arthur, I know, is a part of her, too. He is her, first and foremost.

In the tired blondeness of the mother, in the simplicity of her expression, the weariness of certain gestures, the use of certain words, it is the son I see. The inheritance is here before me, real, physical, terribly physical.

Then, though I do not know it yet, our thoughts, hers and mine, move together towards the same point. We are thinking of the father. It is the father I seek in every detail of Arthur's face which is not his mother's. And it is to the father that she leads me when she makes clear her intention to reveal her terrible secret to me.

What she says, exactly, is: I should tell you when I last saw him, for the first time since his adolescence, he began to ask questions about his father. She says this calmly, because from the beginning she knew she would come to this point. She says this as though it followed logically from what had gone before. She says this as one who expects to find relief in the words. Her face is more resolute, her eyes fix on a point somewhere to my left, her voice becomes more detached as though she were about to recite a text she has learned by heart. And, of course, I imagine she has been over each word a hundred times in her head, that these words are like a stone worn smooth by time, each corner rounded, weathered until it can fit in the palm of one's hand. This stone is her life.

She says, though I have revealed nothing: I know what you're thinking. You're thinking: at last, she's ready to tell her story, she knows it by heart, she has tried to forget it, to wipe it out, but she was soon forced to accept that this was impossible, so she carried her story with her, set it in a corner of her mind and deter-mined to be silent, to suppress it. But suppressing it means it is always on her mind, it grows and grows until it takes up every space, until she courts madness. She knows that she must stay silent even if it means mad-ness. And that is what I have done until today: I stayed silent and in doing so I found myself on the edge of madness. I nearly lost my son to it, and, in the end, I lost him anyhow. I'm sure this all seems a little strange doesn't it, a little absurd? Incomprehensible, certainly. But that is because you don't know what shame is. You don't know, do you? It is something you have never felt. Not the passing shame of some trivial lie, some minor betrayal, some small humiliation. But a shame which overwhelms you, which crushes you, which envelops you until finally it becomes you. When I look back over the last twenty years, shame is what I think of first, shame above everything, shame poisoning everything, infecting everything. And at the moment of telling you the truth, it is this shame I feel, with my whole body, with every fibre of my being. A shame that will never go away.

I want to say to her: don't tell me anything. You don't have to talk to me. You have every right to stay silent. And besides, you're right; why should you speak to me? But I know it would be useless, that she has not come all this way to stop now. And so I let her continue. I feel anxious now and ill at ease. My body starts to shake once more. I measure how I feel by how my body reacts.

She says: you need to imagine the freezing winter of 1894. It was bitterly cold, and it seemed as though it might never end. It was deathly cold – I saw as many bodies that winter as a soldier sees on a battlefield. They were piled up in the streets. Sometimes it took us days to collect them. I lived with my mother near the porte des Lilas. It was a dreary building, but I liked it. An elderly teacher lived next door; it was through him I discovered French literature. To me, the porte des Lilas is, above all, Jean-Jacques Rousseau, Victor Hugo, and the poetry of Arthur Rimbaud. We had arrived in Paris ten years earlier, after my father died. My mother did some cleaning here and there to support us. And then my mother fell ill. A terrible fever that couldn't be treated. Two weeks later, she was dead. She wasn't even forty-five. I found myself alone. They put me out on the street because I was too young, and I didn't have money for the rent. There, now you know: I was twenty years old and in that bitter winter, I was living on the streets. I don't want you to pity me. It was a long time ago, and I was no worse off than a lot of girls my age. Poverty is something to be shared. But it is not something one flaunts.

I think: there is still time to leave, to run away, to escape this story, I can still escape. But I don't run. I stay. I stay to listen to the rest of the story. I have a feeling that it will turn my whole life upside down.

She says: her name was Gisèle. It's a lovely name. If I had had a daughter, I would have called her Gisèle. She looked like a little animal. Her face was sprinkled with freckles, like a child's. She wasn't even twenty. Sometimes we're drawn to people without knowing why, but we know we must go to them, talk to them. I was drawn to Gisèle, though she had done nothing to encourage me. I imagined she might be a companion in adversity, and she certainly was. We told each other our life stories as though we had known one another for years. In the end, she said simply: I've found a way out of all this. All we have to do is trade on our bodies, since that's all we've got left. Twenty years later, that phrase still rings in my ears, I can hear every inflection in it. It's not the sort of phrase you forget.

I realise the direction the story is taking. I know where we are headed. I am sixteen, black hair, green eyes; my name is Vincent de l'Étoile and I know where this woman, who is forty but looks sixty, who is a governess by profession, is leading me. Where she goes, I follow.

I look at her: she is twenty. I look at her: she is blonde, her skin is soft, she looks weary, she is frightened. I look at her: she walks through the door which Gisèle holds open for her, she walks through the door straight into hell, trying to escape another hell. It is early spring, cold April weather, behind her she leaves the trees trembling in the wind, a poor but dignified childhood, some illusions, perhaps, and she enters the counterfeit warmth of an old bourgeois home that has been converted into a brothel. She has come to sell her body, for that is all she has left.

I think of the courage it takes, of the desperation it presupposes. It is like a chasm. I contemplate the abyss.

Then suddenly she is once again a woman of forty who looks sixty. She closes her eyes. She speaks in silence. Suddenly, I see the weight of the years, the weight of the shame. I see her face, crumpled, destroyed, her body heavy, her hair untied, her whole being shapeless, devastated. I understand everything.

She says: they were very kind to me, they welcomed me as one welcomes a new guest. Their kindness was repugnant. I think I would have preferred it if they had been coarse, brutal. That kindness was the real cruelty.

I think of Victor Hugo, the books I read with the old

schoolmaster. I think of the Thènardiers. I think that life is more cruel than literature.

She says: I remember I saw him as he came in. He looked as oriental as I was blond. His face as oval as my body was slender. His appearance as aristocratic as mine was common. His terror as great as mine. I did not despise him for what he was. I despised him for everything he represented. But I thought: better he than another, better this terrified young man than some old dotard. I imagined then that there were many degrees of disgust. I was wrong.

A man to whom you give your body for money is simply a man to whom you give your body for money. Nothing more. It is pointless to deceive yourself. You can look for excuses, there are none. You can try to mitigate the fault, it's a delusion. In the end, nothing remains but what you've done, what you've allowed to be done, what you've been reduced to doing. Nothing else counts for anything. The filth, the warm flesh, the crudeness, the shame wash over everything, fill every space. Perhaps there are women who succeed in coming to terms with it, who can live with this, who can accept it, but I have never met such a woman, nor was I one.

No doubt there are those who have no moral values. Who knows, perhaps such people are right. In any case, they certainly live well.

I could say to her: I am one such, I have no moral values, I do not understand what such values might be, but my words would be inaudible. I do not understand what offence has been committed, though I can gauge the measure of the pain the offence has caused this woman. But she would not understand. And then, despite the shock I know it will create, I hear myself say this: I have no moral values. The words come though I am not master of them. The words come, though I know the mother cannot understand, though I know that they may destroy the trust she has placed in me. And, in fact, her expression changes sharply. She looks at me, her expression signalling her disappointment, her censure. Her expression signals that she was mistaken to have chosen to confide in me. Her whole being shrivels. I must admit that there is an offence, otherwise her expiation is meaningless. If I am not shocked, I cannot understand this story, this shame, this ordeal she has lived. I feel that the conversation will end here, a landslide has come between us; something has been destroyed which cannot be rebuilt. Therefore, to try to save this last bond before it disappears completely, I say: Arthur loved that in me. That among other things. He loved my indifference to the world, my ability to remain untouched by anything, which is one of the purest forms of freedom. That is what it is: Arthur loved me for my freedom. I can tell at once that what I have said has hit the mark, that speaking of her son, of his love for me, has recreated the bond between us. Suddenly, we remember that what brings us together, what binds us, is this death between us. We can feel the dead man's presence between us. We are together once more, she and I. And she begins to accept me for what I am, begins to see her life through another's eyes. She gains some small freedom.

She picks up the thread of her tale: he was a young man of twenty-three. I discovered that later. At first, he said almost nothing. Beneath those grand airs of his, he was dreadfully frightened. I remember thinking that he seemed unused to such establishments, that perhaps for him, too, this was a first time. Secretly, I hoped for a measure of solidarity, of compassion. But I was mistaken: it was with such establishments that he was unfamiliar, not with women. I first sensed this in his clumsiness, in his brusque awkward manner, his forced self-confidence which quickly disintegrated into an almost hysterical fear, the impression he gave of being out of place, of not quite knowing why he was there, of wanting to flee. Yet, at the same time, this young man had a fierce desire to stay, to hold out, to follow to the bitter end some absurd logic, clearly imposed on him by others. So he completed his task conscientiously, pitifully, in the most cursory fashion, as one might discharge a duty. Needless to say I was petrified and consequently less than accommodating. We made a piteous couple. That is what I remember: our wretchedness, our awkwardness. It was an utter fiasco.

Afterwards, he felt the need to speak, not so much to justify himself, nor to apologise, but to confess. What he seemed to need was someone who would listen, someone who could sympathise, but also someone to whom he could admit the truth, safe in the knowledge they would never tell a soul. He had quickly confessed that he had little taste for women and little experience of the physical act. He admitted that he masturbated habitually, what he called his 'bad habit'. He added that it was his father who had given him money to go to a brothel. Listening to him, I began to cry, though I did not know if I was crying for him or for myself. Whatever the truth of the matter, this hurried embrace and this intimate confession had left me feeling permanently sullied. I dressed as soon as the young man had left, rushed downstairs and ran out into the street; I never set foot in that brothel again, nor in any other. My prostitution began and ended there, but more than twenty years later it is those few hours which most haunt me when I sleep.

I know you claim to have no moral values, but I would not blame you if you felt disgusted. Your censure would be as nothing compared to the disgust I have felt for myself for all these years.

I look at her, overcome by shame. I think again of the courage it must take to consent to something she believes to be the most humiliating thing a woman can do. I think especially of the courage it must take to make such a confession. It is an abnegation, a loss of self. At that precise moment, the intimacy between us is absolute. A young man and a woman of forty could not be closer than we are at this moment. What has happened is unbelievable.

I long for the story to be ended, finished, for there to be nothing more to hear, no more blows to suffer, but clearly the secret has not yet been disclosed. This nightmare must be followed to its conclusion.

She says: six weeks later, I realised I was expecting a child. She says this as though it relates to someone other than herself, she says it in a voice that seems detached, distant, almost clinical. I presume it is the only way she can say such a thing without being wracked with sobs, that this reserve is the only means she has of not falling to pieces. I presume, too, that this unexpected, illegitimate child is of necessity the logical outcome, the appalling logic, of this 'utter fiasco', that it is the price that must be paid. The price to pay.

Can a child ever be the price to pay?

She says: that young man is the father, there can be no doubt. He is the only man who could be the father. How could you possibly admit this to your own child? On his birth certificate, I had them write: father unknown.

Arthur was born in Saint-Villier, a village in the south-west, where my mother's family comes from. No one ever mentioned the disgrace of my pregnancy. The child was born into silence, under a blanket of cloud. We returned to Paris when he was learning to walk. It was then that I went into service with your parents.

You are probably wondering why I kept the child. There was an angel-maker, a backstreet abortionist who well knew how to wield her knitting needles. It would have been easy to be rid of the child. Perhaps it would have been for the best. But I simply could not do it. There are some things that one cannot force. I couldn't do it. I couldn't do it.

She says: I do not regret any of it. Of course, I would have been spared the years of disgrace, I would have been spared the suffering I feel today, but I would have been spared, too, the happiness, those years of incomparable happiness.

That phrase is a revelation to me. Of course it is only the memory of her happiness which makes it possible to accept her suffering now, live with it rather than die of it. And then, in the silence, I hear the laughter, see the bodies roll on the bed, the shared looks, the languorous kisses, the soothing tiredness, the promises heard yet unspoken, the fierce radiance of this triumphant summer. Happiness, yes.

We did not have the time to be unhappy together.

To the mother, I say: we had nothing but happiness. I want you to know that. Happiness filled every space between us. It is often like that in the frenzy of those first days. But they were not the first days. They were our days. The seven days I spent with Arthur was the only time we had together, it was a whole life together.

We will not grow old together. That is something else, which has little to do with time.

She weeps. For the first time she weeps. They are soft, almost peaceful tears, something cleansing. As she weeps, she does not take her eyes from me. Her tearful eyes are on me, they never leave me. They thank me.

A long time passes before she speaks again, as in the reverential silence of a church. And then, she says: I must finish my story, I have to tell you what you do not yet know, what is missing. She says: we are at the point where your story and mine come together by the most bizarre coincidence. She says: you know Arthur's father. She says: your friend, Marcel, is Arthur's father.

An explosion. And, in a second, a torrent of images: the young man of twenty-three, an oval face with an oriental cast, an aristocratic bearing; the young man who does not care for women and who goes to a brothel because he is compelled to; the solitary young man, the onanist, inconsolable. The improbable father unaware of his paternity. The homosexual father whose traits I recognise in those of his son. The friend who does not advise me against the love of boys, but who warns me against the love of this boy, his son. The pacifist who loses his loved ones to war. In a second, as in the instant before death, so they say, everything comes back. An explosion.

Could she have lied?

The mother's eyes fix me still, but her tears have dried. In their place, there is an expression that is both calm and terrible. She has taken her confession to its end. She has said all there is to say. She is relieved. She has done her duty.

She sits there, unmoving, weary. She has finished. She, she has finished. For me it has only begun.

Now I am alone, utterly alone. Stop for a moment and try to measure the enormity of my solitude. All I have for company is a secret which weighs on me, and the pain of loss, the knowledge that what awaits me cannot equal what I have already known. There is his absence like a wound, an amputation, the outward sign of something incomplete which can never be made whole. That is the greatest loss. If I think of this as a game of pitch and toss, I can never win more than I have lost. Why play, then? And yet, I cannot remain indifferent. And yet, to desire another is inconceivable. There is no hope for me with men.

For her, it is finished. For me it has just begun.

I shall not write to you again. This is my last letter. I am leaving.

I am leaving because I must, because I cannot do otherwise, because I cannot escape the truth.

I am leaving to shake off the deafening silence, the slow death, the terrible mediocrity; to escape the war which is the cause of my grief, the mud, childhood, family, the earth, all the ties that bind, everything that holds one back.

I am leaving because as this foul and rainy autumn takes hold, I need to find sunlight. Clear waters.

I dream of Italy, of Africa, of the Orient. I dream of exile. I dream of scaling mountains, crossing great plains, treacherous lakes, quiet countryside. I dream of walking to the sea, of journeying deep into desert lands, endless landscapes. I dream of coming to the far-flung reaches of a continent, to the ends of the earth, to the point where all bearings are lost. I dream of indecipherable languages, of suffocating heat, of strange vistas, of ominous clamour, of beautiful light.

I dream that I may think of nothing, searching in the emptiness for a kind of peace.

I can guess what troubles await me, not least the need to survive, accepting the vilest occupations simply to live one day more, wandering among beggars in the foul alleys of strange cities, breaking stones to build churches deep in the desert, risking madness. I fear none of these things. I accept all of these things. Better yet, I long for them. I think that hardship and uncertainty are the only things which might save me.

You can do nothing, Marcel. You perhaps less than anyone else cannot keep me here.

I carry my dead with me.

I take him on this journey from which I will not return except perhaps in death.

Lie With Me

Just outside a hotel in Bordeaux, Philippe, a famous writer, chances upon a young man who bears a striking resemblance to his first love. What follows is a look back to Philippe's teenage years, to a winter morning in 1984, a small French high school, and a carefully timed encounter between two seventeen-year-olds. It's the start of a secret, intensely passionate, world-altering love affair between Philippe and his classmate, Thomas.

Dazzlingly rendered by Molly Ringwald, the acclaimed actor and writer, in her first-ever translation, Besson's exquisitely moving coming-of-age story captures the tenderness of first love – and the heart-breaking passage of time.

'Stunning and heart-gripping'
André Aciman

'A beautiful, shattering novel about desire and shame, about passionate youth and the regrets of age'
Olivia Laing

'It has been years since anything moved me as much as *Lie With Me*. It will become a classic'
Jonathan Coe

The Moustache
Emmanuel Carrère
Translated by Lanie Goodman

One morning, a man shaves off his long-worn moustache, hoping to amuse his wife and friends. But when nobody notices, or pretends not to have noticed, what started out as a simple trick turns to terror. As doubt and denial bristle, and every aspect of his life threatens to topple into madness, a disturbing solution comes into view, taking us on a dramatic flight across the world.

Class Trip
Emmanuel Carrère
Translated by Linda Coverdale

Little Nicolas is a delicate, timid schoolboy, with an excitable, if morbid imagination – the child of an overbearing father. So, two weeks away on the class ski trip is already enough to fill him with dread. But when a child goes missing, Nicolas' mind turns to gruesome possibilities. Compelled to take on the role of detective he edges closer to a truth more shocking than his fears.

The Search Warrant
Patrick Modiano
Translated by Joanna Kilmartin

Haunted by the fate of Dora Bruder – a fifteen-year-old girl listed as missing in an old December 1941 issue of *Paris Soir* – Nobel Prize-winning author Patrick Modiano sets out to find all he can about her. From her name on a list of deportees to Auschwitz to the fragments he is able to uncover about the Bruder family, Modiano delivers a moving survey of a decade-long investigation that revived for him the sights, sounds and sorrowful rhythms of occupied Paris. And in seeking to exhume Dora Bruder's fate, he in turn faces his own family history.

Revenge
Yoko Ogawa
Translated by Stephen Snyder

Murderers and mourners, mothers and children, lovers and innocent bystanders – locked in the embrace of an ominous and darkly beautiful web, their fates all converge through the eleven stories here in Yoko Ogawa's *Revenge*. As tales of the macabre pass from character to character – an aspiring writer, a successful surgeon, a cabaret singer, a lonely craftsman – Ogawa provides us with a slice of life that is resplendent in its chaos, enthralling in its passion and chilling in its cruelty.

@VINTAGEBOOKS

By Night in Chile
Roberto Bolaño
Translated by Chris Andrews

During the course of a single night, Father Sebastian Urrutia
Lacroix – Chilean priest, literary critic and mediocre poet
– relives some of the crucial events of his life. Labouring
under the belief he is dying and in feverish delirium, various
characters, both real and imaginary, appear to him as icy
monsters, as if in sequences from a horror film. Thus we are
given glimpses of the great poet Pablo Neruda, the German
writer Ernst Junger, General Pinochet, whom Father Lacroix
instructs in Marxist doctrine, as well as various members
of the Chilean intelligentsia whose lives, during a period of
political turbulence, have touched upon his.

The Door
Magda Szabó
Translated by Len Rix

Emerence is a domestic servant – strong, fierce, eccentric,
and with a reputation for being a first-rate housekeeper.
When Magda, a young Hungarian writer, takes her on she
never imagines how important this woman will become to
her. It takes twenty years for a complex trust between them
to be slowly, carefully built. But Emerence has secrets and
vulnerabilities beneath her indomitable exterior which will
test Magda's friendship and change the complexion of both
their lives irreversibly.

penguin.co.uk/vintage